# Tell Us
# Your Secret

# Tell Us
# Your Secret

## Barbara Cohen

BANTAM BOOKS
NEW YORK · TORONTO · LONDON · SYDNEY · AUCKLAND

For Sam, Stephanie, Alissa, Amanda,
Kelly, Katie, Heather, Patty,
Laura, Gene, Tess, Kirk,
Kim, Kristin, Erica,
and Mike.

TELL US YOUR SECRET

*A Bantam Book / May 1989*

*The Starfire logo is a registered trademark of Bantam Books, a division of Bantam Doubleday Dell Publishing Group, Inc. Registered in U.S. Patent and Trademark Office and elsewhere.*

**Library of Congress Cataloging-in-Publication Data**

Cohen, Barbara.
Tell us your secret.

Summary: A group of aspiring teenage authors attend a two-week writers' conference where they not only learn about each other but begin to reveal their secret selves.
[1. Interpersonal relations—Fiction.
2. Friendship—Fiction. 3. Authorship—Fiction] I. Title.
PZ7.C6595Te 1989 [Fic] 88-35080
ISBN 0-553-05810-X

*Published simultaneously in the United States and Canada*

PRINTED IN THE UNITED STATES OF AMERICA

FG    0 9 8 7 6 5 4 3 2 1

# First Sunday

The other kids looked normal enough. But they must be real weirdos. Crunch was sure of that. Otherwise what would they be doing here?

Just let the two weeks go fast, he thought. That was all that mattered to him. Just let his sentence be over before he turned into someone as weird as they.

At least the food was all right, so far. They were serving steak for the opening cookout. Hudson Manor was a private school. Maybe they always served steak at private schools. Crunch attended Washington High School in Lenape, New Jersey, where you got hot dogs only on a very good day, like maybe if the governor was visiting.

He couldn't eat steak standing up, not even if he'd had the use of both his arms. He surveyed the two large round tables that had been set up on the veranda of Marygrove, the huge stone mansion in the middle of the Hudson

1

Manor campus. He counted four guys to eight girls, not a bad ratio when you considered that several of the girls were pretty good-looking, for weirdos. He sat down next to the one he regarded as the most promising, a green-eyed blonde named Didi. She smiled at him. "You're Charles, right?"

"Crunch, please. Everyone calls me Crunch."

"What are you, a wrestler?"

"Yeah, as a matter of fact I am. But the name came long before the wrestling. I've been Crunch since I was three."

Didi tapped his cast. "It looks like you're the one who got crunched."

He laughed. "You should see the other guy."

Didi regarded him speculatively for a moment, and then she laughed too.

"Actually," he said, "I broke my arm working out. I fell off the parallel bars."

"No mat?"

"Oh, the mat was there. I just fell funny. I really did a job. This arm is fractured in three places. What about you? Why are you here?"

"What do you mean, why am I here? I'm here to write, of course."

Of course. To Didi, his question must have sounded dumb. Only he could know the logical connection between it and his broken arm. But before he had time to explain, Kent Meckler, at the other table, stood up and raised his hand for silence.

All heads turned toward the director of the Hudson Manor Writers' Conference. "How do you do?" he'd said, holding out his hand to each of them in turn as they'd arrived to register. "Please call me Kent." Crunch won-

2

dered if calling teachers by their first names was a peculiar private-school custom, like steak barbecues.

"We're all here now," Kent was saying, "and I want to take this opportunity to welcome you officially to the 1988 conference. I wish you all an exciting and fruitful two weeks. I hope when it's over you'll find that you've grown as writers, and as human beings."

"We'll grow by about ten pounds if the food's like this every night," a dark-haired boy called out. He wore a white sweatshirt with his name, Danny, imprinted above a small gold and black shield emblazoned with the letters NYCD. New York Cop Department perhaps?

"Don't worry, it won't be," said the boy who'd cooked the steaks on grills.

"Thanks for the warning, Stu." Kent seemed to really know this boy. Maybe he was a student at Hudson Manor they'd hired to help with the cookout. Crunch hoped he was also attending the conference. Four guys to eight girls was a favorable ratio. Three guys to eight girls could get a little lonely. Besides, with his broad shoulders, lively brown eyes, and crooked grin, Stu looked like a regular guy, someone with whom Crunch could hang out.

"Now, I'd like you to meet our workshop leader," Kent continued. "I will be attending all your sessions, and assisting in any way that I can, but as you know, our leader is always a well-known published writer. I don't need to repeat our leader's distinguished biography, since it appears in the preconference material you all received. I will just say, it is a privilege, a pleasure, and an honor to introduce you to Enid Baswell."

Crunch had never heard of Enid Baswell before his mother had thrown the brochure describing the Hudson

3

Manor Writers' Conference on his desk a mere two weeks before. But then, how many writers had he heard of, altogether? He joined politely in the applause initiated by Kent.

Enid Baswell appeared to be in her early forties. A dramatic streak of white highlighted her long, dark, wavy hair. Her clear white skin, large pale-blue eyes, and delicate nose and chin were untouched by makeup. She was dressed like an aging hippie in a tie-dyed T-shirt, a jean skirt, and leather sandals. She smiled all the time, even, as Crunch was to learn, when she was making chopped liver out of a piece of writing. Her speech was brief. "We'll know each other very well by the time this conference is over," she said. "We'll be sharing our writing, so, inevitably, we'll reveal ourselves. But right now we don't know each other at all, and it's very hard to trust strangers enough to read to them things that you've written. So let's just go around the room and say our names and where we're from, and then I have a little writing exercise that may help us get to know one another a little bit. I'm Enid Baswell. You'll call me Enid. I live in Manhattan now, but I was born and raised in Blue Creek, West Virginia."

She wasn't wasting any time. She nodded to Kent, who was sitting next to her. "Kent Meckler," he said. "I'm chairman of the English department here at Hudson Manor, as well as founder and director of the Hudson Manor Writers' Conference. I was born in East Lansing, Michigan, and brought up in Dade County, Florida." Florida hadn't rubbed off on him, Crunch thought. But then, neither had Michigan. He looked and even sounded a little like a British clergyman on an episode of *Masterpiece Theater*.

4

The others rattled off identifying information. James Birmingham, of Baltimore, had just graduated from Penns Landing, a prep school in Bucks County, Pennsylvania. Martina Cole was entering her sophomore year at Boston Latin. "That sounds like a private school," she said, "but it isn't."

"Oh, my school is private," Sierra McCaughey of Sacramento, California, interjected. "We have only about twenty-five in a class. To get in, you have to pass about five thousand tests. It's awfully selective. I mean, the competition is fierce. Kids have nervous breakdowns."

Stu Llewellyn was both a workshop member and the only regular Hudson Manor student at the conference. NYCD stood for New York Collegiate Day, where Danny Epstein would be a junior. Rhonda Tulipano of Burlington, Vermont, attended a public school. She, like Crunch and most of the others, was entering her senior year. Crunch announced himself as Crunch Oliver of Lenape, New Jersey. "I was christened Charles," he explained, "but when I hear it, I think you're talking to my father."

Didi from Cos Cob, Connecticut, wasn't the only looker. Linda Kelly of Shawnee Mission, Kansas, and Eve Streitman, a sophomore at Maimonides Hebrew Day School in Manhattan, offered her some competition. Crunch dismissed Meg Eriksson and Beth Miller, both from Shaker Heights, outside of Cleveland. They just weren't his type.

Enid nodded in Beth's direction. "I see you've got your notebook with you. Good. The rest of you—from now on, I never want to see you without a notebook. That goes for you too, Kent."

"Even in bed?" Kent asked.

"I don't intend to see you when you're in bed," Enid replied through her smile.

5

Kent blushed, but then he grinned too. A faint ripple of laughter moved among the kids.

Enid reached into a large canvas knapsack and pulled out some paper and pencils. "Just this once, I'll supply you. Someone want to give me a hand?"

Sierra was on her feet instantly. The apple-polisher. The blackboard-cleaner. There isn't a class without one, Crunch thought, even when the class contains only a dozen kids. Sierra passed out the supplies while Enid continued talking. "I want you each to write down what's in your room at home. Just a list, containing as many items as you can recall." That didn't sound very difficult. Crunch felt as if a weight he hadn't even known he was carrying had slipped from his shoulders, for the time being at least.

"What's the sense of this?" James asked.

"Trust me," Enid said. "Don't write your names on the papers."

Everyone immediately started scribbling, Enid and Kent included. James, sitting opposite Crunch, was moving his pencil too, but he wasn't writing anything. He was drawing.

Crunch steadied his paper with his cast. "Bed," he wrote. "Dresser. Mirror. Desk. Blinds. Carpet." That was the most boring list he'd ever seen. He decided to improve upon it. He put a comma after "carpet" and wrote, "very old, stained with ink, coffee, beer, and dog pee." That was better. "Stereo. About nine thousand records, mostly by the Grateful Dead. Weight lifting equipment. TV. Red telephone for calling girls. A pile of old *Playboy* magazines. Formal portrait, framed, of the 1985 New York Rangers. Books." Should he name some titles? No, that might give away too much. "Sprawled on the bed, a

6

lazy, lovable Labrador named Lil." Once he got started, he couldn't stop. "A cigar box full of kid stuff I can't throw away, including a Boy Scout penknife, a packet of baseball cards, two shooters, a Mondale for President button . . ." By the time Enid called a halt, his list covered one whole side of paper, and half the other side.

"Okay," Enid said, "fold your papers in half and hand them to me." She shuffled them, and passed them out again, making sure no one got his or her own back. "Let's read these lists out loud. Let's see if we can make any guesses about the kind of person who lives in that room. Anyone want to start?"

Again Sierra waved her hand in the air. But Enid didn't call on her. "How about you, Rhonda?" she asked. Had Enid remembered all their names from just one go-round? Or had she called on Rhonda because hers was the only name she *did* remember?

Rhonda read out the list in her hand. "Obviously a girl," she said when she was done.

"How do you know?" Enid asked.

"Makeup on the dresser. A collection of dolls from foreign countries."

Meg glanced at Beth. "She's a real intellectual, or at least she wants us to think that she is." Nearly six feet tall, Meg exuded the almost insolent confidence of a Viking princess.

"How do you know that?" Enid queried.

"The books. Look at those titles she listed. *War and Peace*. *Zen and the Art of Motorcycle Maintenance*. What happened to the twenty-seven Barbara Cartland romances? I notice she didn't mention them."

7

"Okay, okay, I should have, I know I should have," Beth exclaimed. "Also the box of Mounds bars in the bottom drawer of the dresser. Even you didn't know about that, did you, Meg? Now let them read yours." She addressed the group. "Hers is the one with the bed bugs. She hasn't changed the sheets since 1983."

Meg poked Beth's arm. Beth poked her back. Rhonda returned Beth's list, and then it was Beth's turn to read the one in her hand. "Only it doesn't say anything," Beth said. She held it up. It was James's drawing, and it didn't represent a room. It was a cartoon of a woman with long hair, a tattered jean skirt, a book in one hand and a pen in the other. James had made no attempt to reproduce Enid's features. Instead he'd given her the face of a long-toothed rabbit. Enid took the drawing from Beth's hand and examined it for a long moment. "Who did it?" she asked.

"Me," James admitted.

"Not a bad likeness," she remarked lightly. "Do you write too?"

"When I feel like it."

"Do you have any idea of the purpose of this exercise I assigned?"

"It's dumb," James responded.

"Someone else?" Enid called out.

"So we can get to know each other," Sierra stated, sounding as if she were Madame Curie announcing the discovery of radium.

Enid nodded. "Yes. I said as much. Any other reason? Anything having to do with the fact that this is a writers' workshop?"

Eve spoke, volunteering a remark for the first time since the exercise had begun. "It's the details," she said.

8

"The specific details. We learn a lot about each other from those lists. And yet they're not descriptions. They're not bunches of adjectives."

Enid smiled, clearly pleased. "Exactly, Eve. Nothing much is conveyed by broad generalities. If I can give you only one message in these two weeks, it's this one: be specific." She turned back to James. "Read the list you've got," she ordered. This time, James obeyed. He had Linda's list, Linda had Stu's, and Stu had Crunch's. While Stu read it, Crunch leaned back in his seat with careful nonchalance.

"An athlete," Didi said when Stu was done. "Obviously."

"An animal lover," Linda added.

"A sex maniac," Meg offered.

"Well, who's paper is it?" Enid asked.

"I have a pretty good idea," Stu said. "I think it's his." He pointed to Crunch.

"Sharp guess," Crunch admitted.

"Accurate?" Enid asked.

"Not bad. The sex maniac part—that's right on."

"Lock your doors, girls," Didi called out.

"Now read the one you're holding," Enid instructed.

Crunch glanced down at the paper in his hand. It was printed in a script so fine that it looked as if it had been drawn rather than written. It wasn't a list. It was a paragraph. "My room is my cave," Crunch read. "I retreat there to soak my feet, nurse my wounds, stretch my mind. The bed is for dreaming, the telephone for gossiping, the rock records for laughs. When I laugh out loud, my father knocks on my door. 'What's the matter, little one?' he asks. 'Are you all right?' Whenever I laugh, he thinks something's wrong. So I switch the stereo to Mo-

9

zart and stare long and hard at the framed print of Van Gogh's *Sunflowers* that hangs on my white wall. And after a while I'm not even mad at my father anymore."

The words Crunch had read seemed to vibrate in the silence. Afterward, when he thought about that first night, he'd imagine that at that moment the lights on the porch had dimmed, an improbable autumnal chill had blown across the lawn, and he'd shivered. But of course that hadn't happened at all. Then he hadn't understood what Eve's paragraph revealed. He'd been as ignorant as a baby.

After a while, Enid spoke. "Anyone have anything to say about this one?"

"Talented," Danny offered.

"*Very* talented," Beth added. It was the first praise she'd offered all evening.

"It's like a story," Martina said. "Only I don't know what it means."

"I think she's kind of mysterious," Danny said. "As if she had a secret."

"How do you know it's a she?" Enid asked.

"The guys' papers have all been read," Crunch pointed out matter-of-factly.

"I'm glad someone's counting the cards," Enid said. "And the other thing, Danny. Why do you call her mysterious?"

"She calls her room her cave. It sounds like she's hiding there."

"Good, Danny. And good, whoever wrote this. Whose is it?"

Eve raised her hand. "What *is* your secret, Eve?" Crunch asked quietly. He gazed at her elfin face surrounded by a cloud of soft black curls. Though no more than five feet tall, her body, clad in a skintight black tank top and a pair of brief pink shorts, appeared to lack none of the essentials.

She smiled and reached toward him for her paper. "I'm addicted to corn chips and root beer."

Crunch held the paper behind his back. "That's it? That's the whole thing?"

"I'm just your average, everyday teenager," Eve said. Her smile seemed somewhat strained now.

Crunch's eyes were fixed on Eve. So were everyone else's. "You have to tell us more," Crunch said, "or you don't get your paper back."

"So keep it." She sat back down in her chair. "A masterpiece it isn't."

"You vant to know *my* secret?" Rhonda murmured in a Greta Garbo voice, as she pulled down the brim of the baseball cap she was wearing so that it shadowed her face.

"Sure," Crunch said.

She gave him a sly look from beneath half-closed lids. "I haf no secret."

"I'm sure you do," Enid said. "Everyone does. Please, hold on to everything you write during this conference—the exercises, the stuff you do on your own, even an assignment as simple as this one. Just as you never know what secret lies behind the most ordinary-looking facade, you never know which casual scribble might provide the kernel for the major project you're going to present the last day we're here."

Crunch felt the weight fall on his shoulders again. A major project. What did that mean? Kent was explaining. Each year the conference published a review containing a lengthy sample of each participant's writing. It could be a short story, an article, a group of poems, or a selection

11

from a longer work in progress. Kent outlined a schedule. First an idea was to be presented, then a rough draft, then a revision, and another, and another, until time ran out. The magazine would be printed over the summer and mailed to them in the fall. I just won't do it, Crunch thought. He hadn't bargained for this. What was the worst punishment they could inflict anyway? Throwing him out? That would actually be a blessing.

The session was over. Enid clapped her hand on James's shoulder, forcing him to listen to whatever it was she was saying to him in a low, intense voice. Kent disappeared inside Marygrove, where, it seemed, he lived. Stu swept paper plates and plastic knives and forks into a garbage bag. The others drifted off the porch and onto the lawn, heading toward the dorms in clumps of two and three.

Crunch caught up with Eve, Martina, and Rhonda. "Eve!" he called. "Your paper."

As she took it from him, he grabbed her wrist. "I'm sorry I didn't give it to you before. I was only teasing."

Martina and Rhonda gazed smilingly at the scene. Crunch was smiling too. It was only Eve who seemed to find nothing amusing in the interchange. "Let go of me!" she said. She drew her breath in sharply and with her free hand clawed at his fist. Such vehemence in one so tiny was surprising, but not, Crunch discovered, utterly unattractive.

Eve continued down the path, alone. "We're going into town after the dorm meeting," Rhonda said. "Look around a little, see if anything's there. You want to come? Who knows what interesting things might develop."

"Maybe we ought to get that guy Stu to come with us too," Crunch suggested. "He knows his way around here."

"Good idea."

12

"I'll ask him." Crunch started back toward Marygrove. Then, as if on a sudden impulse, he turned again to Rhonda. "Is Didi coming?"

"We were going to ask her."

"Eve?"

"She said she'll see, after the meeting."

Crunch found Stu folding up the chairs and the tables. There'd be another cookout the last night, but in the meantime they'd take the rest of their meals in the dining room. "You want to go into town with us later?" Crunch asked. "We could use someone who's familiar with the place."

Stu nodded. "Sure. It's definitely a one-horse town, but what little action there is, I know about."

"I'd help you, if I could," Crunch apologized.

"It's all right. I'm getting paid. I mean, I'm getting to come to the conference for free by doing stuff like this."

"You must want to be here awful bad."

"It beats lifeguarding."

"Yeah?" Stiff-armed, Crunch waved the cast reaching well above his elbow at Stu. "If it weren't for this, that's exactly what I'd be doing. Lifeguarding on Long Beach Island. Oceans of gorgeous girls in bikinis. If you ask me, it sure beats this place."

"A couple of the girls around here aren't bad. Like Linda."

Crunch picked up two folding chairs with his good hand. "She's not bad at all. I'll tell you what. I'll stay away from her, if you'll leave me Didi and Eve. I haven't decided which one it's going to be." He followed Stu inside. "Rhonda's kind of interesting too."

"Yeah," Stu said as he piled chairs beneath the curving

13

marble staircase that dominated Marygrove's huge foyer. "But she's not exactly a ten."

"Looks aren't everything." Crunch laid the chairs he was carrying on top of Stu's pile. "I mean, going out with a ten doesn't make me any happier than going out with a nine and three quarters." Stu laughed. Crunch lifted his head and stared up at the gilded ceiling soaring thirty feet above his head. "This building is a ten."

"On the outside," Stu returned. "But it's falling apart. A weird old millionaire named Erastus Grove built it for his wife Mary. She was much younger than he, and they never had any kids. Later they started the school. Once Hudson Hall got built, the mansion wasn't used for classes anymore. The upstairs was turned into apartments, and they rent the downstairs out for weddings and stuff. If they didn't do that, they couldn't afford to keep it up at all."

The huge stone building was as fanciful as a fairy-tale castle, with carved stonework decorating the ivy-covered exterior, and unmatched chimneys, cupolas, dormers, and incongruous TV antennas scattered helter-skelter over the tiled roof. The hall in which Stu and Crunch now stood was dim and empty of furniture except for two giant-sized tattered chairs drawn up by the largest marble fireplace Crunch had ever seen. More marble, stone, and magnificent inlaid wood were everywhere, though barely visible now in the deepening twilight. "This is a good house for a ghost," Crunch said.

"One lives here, of course," Stu replied. "One or two. Maybe more."

"Whose?"

"Erastus Grove's, at least. He died one summer in

14

Europe. Mary had his body embalmed and dragged it all the way back here on a boat. There's a marker for him on a grave in the Holy Innocents Episcopal churchyard, but there's a rumor that Mary secretly buried him right here in the cellar, because he loved the place so much."

"Ever been down in that cellar?" Crunch asked. Cellars, or attics, often played major roles in the horror novels he loved to read.

"I've been in the storerooms under the kitchen. That's all. There's another whole section that doesn't connect to the main part."

"Maybe I could write a ghost story," Crunch said. "I mean, if I really *have* to write something."

Stu pushed open the heavy oak door and the two of them stepped back out onto the porch. "What are you doing here, anyway, Crunch?" he asked. "I mean, if you're not interested in writing?"

"My mom made me come," Crunch explained. "She found out about it from the guidance counselor, filled out the application, even drove me here. The only way I could have avoided coming would have been to run away from home, and I'm in no condition to do that." He glanced ruefully at his cast. "She and my dad had planned this trip to Italy. They didn't want to give it up, and they absolutely refused to let me stay home alone."

"But you must write because you had to submit a writing sample to get admitted here. Where did it come from? Did your mother make that up too?" Stu hoisted himself up on the low wall beneath one of the vaulting Gothic arches that alternated with Greek columns to form the porch of Marygrove.

Crunch leaned against a column. "She wouldn't lie. She

15

sent in a poem of mine that appeared in the school literary magazine. I wrote it when I was a freshman. It was an assignment, and my teacher submitted it. I suffered on account of that thing. For weeks the guys called me Percy—as in Percy Bysshe Shelley. You can be sure I never wrote another one." That *was* a lie. He had written three more poems. They'd been about girls. He just hadn't shown them to anyone, certainly not to any English teachers. And certainly not to the girls. Marla Romano. Antoinette Schaeffer. Ducky Alpaugh. They were not the willing classmates he dated. They were older girls, haunting girls, inaccessible girls, girls who inspired inexpressible confusions he'd tried to exorcise in those poems. Girls a little like Eve, Crunch thought. Of course, she was younger than he, not older, but she too appeared inaccessible, at least so far. Whether or not she was really so hard to get remained to be seen.

"That must be one helluva poem," Stu said.

"I don't know. Maybe."

"I've never written any poetry. I hope Enid doesn't make us do poems. I write adventure stuff. I'm working on a novel about an outlaw named Albrecht. It's really great. Someone gets killed on just about every page." Stu glanced at his watch and then slid down from his perch. "Hey, it's nearly eight. We better get over to that dorm meeting."

"Okay." Crunch straightened up. "By the way, before we go—how do you get into the cellar? The other part, that doesn't connect with the kitchen storerooms."

"You planning to visit Erastus Grove's secret tomb?"

"If I end up writing that ghost story, I'll need, you know, some background." Lenape, New Jersey, seemed

16

singularly devoid of scary locations. Even the graveyards had an everyday familiarity about them. Crunch thought he'd like to lay eyes on a place like the ones Stephen King seemed to stumble on almost daily.

"I guess there must be an inside passage somewhere," Stu said. "The person who'd know for sure is Dobkin. He's the custodian and of course he hates anybody under fifty. But there's an outside cellar door too, and it might lead to that other section. Come on, I'll show you." He led Crunch around to the side porch, where wide, shallow steps led down to the drive. He pushed aside the thick growth of rhododendron covering the foundation and pointed out an angled metal cellar door, the kind kids fifty or sixty years ago used to slide on. The handles were secured by a rusted padlock.

"I suppose Dobkin has the key," Crunch said.

"Unless it was lost back in the Ice Age," Stu returned. "Come on, we better get going."

They made their way across the wide, oak-shaded lawn that separated Marygrove from the main campus. Crunch noticed that Stu's stride was as firm and athletic as his own, and the muscles on his tanned forearms as well-developed. "Hey, Stu," Crunch asked, "what's your sport?"

"I wrestle some," Stu replied diffidently.

"Hey, me too."

Stu nodded. Crunch smiled. There was at least one guy to hang out with. There were two girls to pursue. And maybe some ghosts to encounter and some mysteries to solve—Rhonda's secret and Eve's and the secret in the cellar of Marygrove. Maybe these two weeks wouldn't be so terrible after all.

17

# First Monday

Eve awoke, trembling. In the gray light of very early morning she saw that the clock on the bedstand read five forty-five. She recognized the clock, but not the bedstand nor the bed nor the room. Where was she? In the confusion of her abrupt awakening, she could not remember.

She had dreamed about the search again. She was rushing to the subway station to meet someone. She didn't know the person's name. She knew only that it was someone she cared about very much. She arrived on the empty platform just as the train was pulling out. Hoping to catch it, she ran like the wind to the next stop, but the same thing happened. She could see the lights on the back of the last car receding down the tracks; the roar of its wheels filled her ears. Once again, no one was waiting for her on the platform. As she desperately hurried from station to station, her panic grew. Her heart was in her

18

throat; she was overwhelmed by a terrible sense of loss. She would never meet the train; the person would never be waiting for her on the platform. It was not merely frustration she felt, but a consuming anguish far greater than a mere description of the situation could possibly account for.

When the pain grew too huge to bear, she'd awaken suddenly, awash with sweat, as she had this morning. Who was this person on the train whom she cared about so much? Her mother? Her father? A beloved friend? Eve could not be sure. If she'd remained in the dream a moment longer, she would have found out. But though some part of her wanted to know, she could not have stayed. The dream was dreadful beyond describing, and her relief at waking up was like the ease one feels when a fever passes.

She shook the tatters of the dream from her head, squeezed her eyes shut, and opened them again. Fully awake, she understood now where she was—in a dormitory at Hudson Manor in Vandyk's Crossing, New York. She was free. It had been a battle, but she'd convinced her parents to let her come. Except for their daily phone call, she was free for two weeks. Well, not quite two weeks. Counting today, twelve days.

She hopped out of bed and leaned out the open window, drawing in deep breaths of the sweet, moist morning air. It was warm for so early; they were in for another hot day. Nothing at Hudson Manor was air-conditioned; it hadn't been built for summer use. But that fact had its advantages. A day camp met on campus, but the only live-in summer program was the writers' conference. More than enough space was available in the dorm that had

19

been opened for their use to provide participants with the private rooms they needed if they were to get any work done.

Eve sat down at her desk and opened a notebook in which she carefully inscribed the name of each conferee (Was there such a word? she wondered) on a separate line. She ruled two vertical columns, one of which she labeled "July 11," the other "July 22." She wrote in the first column.

July 11

James Birmingham.     Professional rebel. What's he doing here? Could be fun.

Martina Cole.     A long, sad face with large, loving brown eyes, like an orphaned puppy. A possible friend.

Meg Eriksson.     Much more mature than the others. Or do I think that because she's so tall? She and her buddy Beth seem to be looking down on the rest of us.

Danny Epstein.     Your normal very smart rich New York kid. Maybe nicer than a lot of them.

Linda Kelly.     Very pretty, very quiet. Haven't formed an opinion about her yet. Does that mean there's more to her than to the others— or less?

20

| | |
|---|---|
| Stu Llewellyn. | Beautiful brown eyes and a wonderful smile. He likes Linda, so does Danny. Who will win? Only Linda knows, and she's not saying. |
| Sierra McCaughey. | An impossible snob. No one can stand her, including me. |
| Beth Miller. | She's very smart, which she makes no pretense of hiding. But I like her. I think she's honest. It's hard to tell though, because she hardly talks to anyone but Meg. |
| Charles "Crunch" Oliver. | Good-looking, and knows it. Comes on to every girl he talks to. I turned him off, but fast. Didi can have him if she wants him. All he talks about is sports and sex. What's he doing here? |
| Eve Streitman. | Will anything happen to her at Hudson Manor, or will she go home the same girl she came? |
| Rhonda Tulipano. | Always wears a hat—three different ones in twelve hours. Friendly and funny, but there's also something strange going on behind her little clown face. |
| Didi Watson. | She and Linda in a close contest for the best-looking girl here. Hair and makeup perfect, terrific clothes. Can she write? |

21

When the conference was over, she'd fill in the second column. It would be interesting to see if first impressions persisted or proved to be entirely mistaken. Somewhere in between, she supposed. It was amazing how much you could learn about people while sharing pizza.

Eve ate breakfast with Martina, Rhonda, and Danny, who wondered out loud at least three different times if Linda was coming. She didn't, and neither did anyone else. But by nine o'clock they'd gathered in the English resource room in the classroom building, Hudson Hall—all of them, except for James. Kent sent Stu back to the dorm to roust him out of bed, and he drifted in around quarter of ten. By this time they'd scattered to comfortable seats beneath windows to work on the task Enid had assigned: "Write a page describing a room so as to reveal the inhabitant's personality without ever naming the person."

Laughing, lighthearted Stu amazed them all by producing a highly original piece. A deformed, evil wizard lived in the room Stu described, and Eve knew it from the first sentence. "Push away the spiderwebs as you enter, but be careful, you don't want the Black Widow to bite you." If this exercise was any indication, Didi, as Eve had suspected, couldn't write, but Eve found herself amused or charmed or surprised by several other efforts. Linda described a bear's cave, and though she never named the animal, there was no doubt who lived there. Even more surprising was Sierra's limpid, golden paragraph about her grandmother's kitchen, but the self-satisfied smile with which she concluded her reading obviated the good effect. Eve could smell the sweat in Danny's funny-sad high school locker room, described from the point of view of a guy who couldn't take two steps without tripping. Crunch wrote about his orthopedist's office.

"Sounds like a medieval torture chamber to me," Martina commented.

Crunch nodded. "You got it. It's the worst place I've ever been. And this broken arm is the worst thing that ever happened to me."

"Then I guess you've led a pretty nice life," Eve commented drily.

"Well, not the worst thing," he amended hastily. "Not *really* the worst thing."

The room in Rhonda's paper kept changing. First it was an ordinary suburban teenager's bedroom, then it was a boudoir in a royal palace, then it was a jail cell, and then it was back to a bedroom again. "This kid is schiz," James said.

"Something like that," Rhonda agreed.

"Is she you?" James asked.

Rhonda shrugged.

James had produced another drawing, this time a caricature of Kent, with the face of a lugubrious donkey. Meg refused to read hers. "It's no good," she said. This didn't mean that she thought the ones that had been read were better than hers. It simply meant that none of them, her own included, met her high standards.

"I need to see it, Meg," Enid said. "Please bring it when we have our conference this afternoon." Her voice brooked no argument, and Meg shrugged a kind of agreement.

Eve was glad her first conference with Enid was not until the following day. Returning to the dorm from a late-afternoon walk with Martina, she heard voices emerging from Stu's room. They wandered in through his open door. Danny was studying the schedule Kent had distributed earlier that day. "Monday, July 11: Harold Stutz, editor and vice president, King Books," he read. "Tuesday, July 12: Dorothy Mannheim, author's agent, Mannheim Associates. Friday, July 15: Gregory Hyde, book review editor, *Predictions* magazine. Saturday, July 16: Trip to New York City for sight-seeing and theater. Monday, July 18: Sylvie Hoving, playwright, author of hit Broadway comedy *Lilacs and Liverwurst*."

"That's enough, Danny," Beth interrupted. "We're all writers, meaning that we probably all know how to read too." It was the first time Eve had seen Beth unaccompanied by Meg.

Danny defended himself. "I was just trying to make a point. This is a good program. They're giving us our money's worth."

"Oh, come off it," Sierra responded. "This is nothing. I mean, who's Sylvie Hoving? Broadway hit? I never even heard of *Lilacs and Liverwurst*."

"That's because you're from California," Beth retorted. "The only name they recognize in California is the one in the center box of *Hollywood Squares*."

"Steven Spielberg spoke to the English classes at Sand Hill this year," Sierra said. "So did Robert DeNiro. So you can't expect me to be impressed by Sylvie Hoving. Or Enid Baswell."

"Basically," Martina offered, "this program is like any other. We'll get out of it what we put into it."

Beth put her arm around Martina. "I love you, Martina. You're so straight." The remark's content conveyed an insult, the tone a compliment.

Crunch, passing by in the hall, poked his head through the doorway. "You guys ready to go over for dinner?"

24

"If it's anything like lunch," Rhonda said, "I think I can skip it." That evening she was wearing a welder's cap perched precariously atop her punk hairdo.

"I warned you last night was a freak," Stu reminded her as he rose to his feet. "But come on, you can't starve. There's always the salad bar." Out in the hall, he rapped briskly on James's door. Meg opened it. Barefoot, she held a cigarette in her hand. Eve sniffed the distinctive smoky, sweet odor that drifted out of the room. "You guys coming to dinner?" Stu queried.

Meg smiled, a relaxed, easy smile. "Soon. Don't wait for us."

"Rory or Beatrice will be poking around before they go over," Stu warned quietly. Rory and Beatrice were the faculty couple who received a free apartment in the dorm in exchange for acting as house parents.

"Thanks, Stu," James called. "Don't worry about it. We can handle Randy Rory and Queen Bea." Meg withdrew, shutting the door behind her. Stu moved on to Linda's room.

Outside, Beth fell in step alongside Eve. "I liked your piece this morning."

"You did? Thanks. I liked yours too."

"You don't have to say that."

"I mean it. Didn't you think it was any good?"

"It was all right, I guess. The level here isn't really very high, is it? Maybe I should have done what Meg did, and not read mine at all."

"Did she write something?"

"Oh, yes, she wrote something. She's very, very good. She's the best one here, I'm sure."

25

"We'll never know, will we, unless she's willing to read to us," Eve remarked softly.

Beth's eyebrows lifted in surprise. "I suppose you're right. I guess maybe Danny comes next to Meg. And then Stu."

"Isn't it too soon to judge? Two exercises, and one just a list?"

"Didi's no good. All those vague adjectives. 'The room was soft and fluffy and feminine and charming.'"

"Maybe she'll learn. Maybe that's why she came."

"Are you always so charitable?"

Eve laughed. "I've already written down my opinions of everyone in my notebook, in ink—on the basis of just one exercise, and an evening in a pizza parlor. But I did leave a column to fill in on the last day. So much for charity."

"Do you think Rhonda really is schiz?"

Eve shook her head. "She *seems* perfectly normal most of the time. But there is something really odd about her. Every once in a while she drops these little hints I can't make head or tail of. Like last night in the pizza parlor when she said she had two mothers and two fathers, but no, her parents weren't divorced. And then she clammed up and wouldn't say another word."

"I couldn't get over Sierra's piece," Beth said. "I wanted to hate it, but I couldn't."

Eve nodded agreement. "Let's face it, the only hopeless one was Didi's. No one knows what James would do if he chose to do it, and you're the only one who knows what Meg can do. So that leaves eight acceptable efforts. I think you're wrong. I think the level here is pretty high."

Crunch caught up with them. "You want to hit some tennis balls after supper?" he asked. Eve was annoyed.

26

She adored the kind of intellectual gossip she was enjoying with Beth. Crunch immediately brought the conversation down to the lowest common denominator—him.

"Who're you inviting?" Beth queried sharply. "Me or Eve?"

"Both of you," Crunch replied genially. "I'll get a fourth. Stu maybe, or Didi."

"How can you play tennis, Crunch?" Eve asked. "You've only got one arm."

"I can do everything but serve. Not well, but I can do it. Listen, I was no Ivan Lendl even before this arm thing, but I've got to let off steam somehow."

"You could run, or walk."

"It's not just exercise. I need competition too."

"Well, I certainly wouldn't provide you with any," Eve assured him. "Count me out."

"Remember, I have only one arm."

"I don't want to." She enunciated each word carefully. Even someone as complacent as Crunch ought to get the message.

"I'll play you," Beth offered. "Maybe if you tied your legs together too, I could take one game out of four."

"Oh, okay. Thanks." Crunch was trying to be gracious, but his face registered disappointment.

What does he want me for? Eve wondered. He probably can get any other girl here, except Meg, perhaps. Maybe that's why. Maybe he's one of those. All he wants is what he can't get. She lengthened her stride to catch up with Martina and Rhonda, leaving Beth and Crunch to walk the rest of the way together.

She was at the salad bar, piling greens and cottage cheese on her plate, when Stu, Linda, and Danny arrived

27

together. "What are you?" Stu wondered. "A rabbit or something?"

"Rabbits don't eat cottage cheese," Linda said.

"Is there anything about animals you don't know?" Stu asked.

"Lots," Linda assured him.

"Kosher, more likely," Danny suggested.

"More likely than what?" Stu asked.

"Eve's more likely kosher than a rabbit."

Eve laughed. "If I were strictly kosher, I wouldn't eat here at all. I'm not kosher, but pork is pushing it." Knockwurst and sauerkraut was the menu for the evening.

The four of them sat down at an empty table where, a few minutes later, Crunch and Beth joined them. "If you're not really kosher," Stu asked, "then why draw the line at pork? You can't think God cares, because if you did, you'd be kosher all the way."

Eve shrugged. "It doesn't have anything to do with God. If for three thousand years my ancestors choked on pork, who am I to start eating it?" There was more to it than that, of course. Stu's question had been framed seriously; Eve felt it deserved an honest answer. "I guess I think about all those Jews, over time, who were forced to swallow food that was an abomination to them, just to stay alive. Maybe I don't eat pork for their sake."

"How can you eat pizza without sausage?" Crunch asked. "It has no taste. You ought to try it sometime; I bet you'd like it."

His remark struck Eve as so profoundly stupid she didn't even bother to frame a reply. "I eat plain pizza all the time," Linda explained. "It's fine. I'm thinking of going veggie anyway." She turned to Stu. "We going back to the pizzeria tonight?"

28

"After we listen to that editor? Sure, why not? Shall we go over right after his talk, or should I pick you up in your room about ten o'clock?"

"Pick me up," Linda said.

That made it a date. Danny glanced from Linda to Stu and back to Linda again. Then he caught Eve studying his response. He smiled a little. "You want to come too?" he asked her. "For plain pizza, of course. I may have a few mushrooms and peppers, but certainly no sausage."

"Are the rest of us included in this expedition?" Crunch asked.

"Sure," Danny replied. "It's a free country." He turned back to Eve. "I'll knock on your door. Ten o'clock."

"Is that all right, Eve?" Crunch asked.

"Of course it's all right," Eve said as she rose from the table. "I'll need a slice of pizza after this nothing supper." She addressed herself very deliberately to Danny. "Ten o'clock, Danny." Then she picked up her tray and walked away.

Danny was okay, Eve thought. She could have pizza with Danny. She could even go out with him, more or less. She'd had plenty of experience with the Dannys of this world. Maimonides Hebrew Day was full of talented, brilliant, funny, insecure, striving, high-strung Dannys. Young Woody Allens, only a little better looking. She felt perfectly safe with them.

# First Tuesday

Enid crossed her jean-clad legs on the desk blotter as she leaned back in her swivel chair. Crunch figured he'd known about fifty teachers fairly well in the course of his life. She was the first one who put her feet up on the desk during a conference. "Listen," he asked, "are you really a teacher or really a writer?"

She laughed. "I'm really both. I can't make a living writing fiction; I have to do some teaching too. But I like it; I'd do it even if I wrote best-sellers. Writing's lonesome. I need to get out and see people every now and then."

"My coming here was kind of—well, kind of sudden. I didn't get a chance to look at anything you've written."

"Try the Vandyk's Crossing Public Library." Suddenly she dropped her legs to the floor and sat up straight. "That's enough about me. What about you? What are you going to do for your big project? Any ideas?"

Crunch folded his arms across his chest. "I'm not much of a writer."

"Who is?"

"What I mean is, I'm different from these other guys." He had to tell her; otherwise she'd expect too much. "The only reason I'm here is because my folks needed to get rid of me for two weeks. I was supposed to be lifeguarding at the beach, but I can't do that with this arm. So they sent me here. Only I can't write."

"You can't? I hadn't noticed."

"Huh?"

"The stuff you do in class is as good as most everyone else's, and better than some. Surely you realize that."

"Are you saying I've got talent?"

"Talent's the least of it. But all the sweat in the world won't compensate for its total absence. You have enough."

"Is that the truth? Or are you just 'encouraging' me— you know, because you're a teacher and because you're supposed to?"

She lifted her hand. "Okay, you got me. I wouldn't tell any kid here he or she was a lousy writer. You're right about that. I'm not in the business of cutting kids up. But I don't lie either."

"All right," Crunch allowed. "You don't lie."

Enid leaned back again. "I don't know everything. In writing even more than in cooking, one man's meat is another man's poison. It's because I don't know every-thing that I don't dare be destructive. But I would never utter a word I didn't feel to be the truth. I care too much about writing to do that."

"So you think I have talent."

"Enough talent, as I said."

31

"Enough for what?"

"Enough to produce ten pages by the end of next week."

"Ten pages of what?"

"That's what I'm asking you."

He scratched his head. "Stu's writing about this outlaw."

Enid nodded.

"That's all right?"

"Of course it's all right. What's wrong with an adventure story?"

"Nothing, so far as I'm concerned."

"Oh. You thought there might be something wrong with it so far as *I'm* concerned."

This time he nodded.

"Crunch, I'm not asking for great literature," Enid said. "I'm just asking for writing. All any of us can do is write. Whether or not it's literature—well, we have to leave that decision to someone else."

"Okay, then." Crunch lifted his chin. "I'm going to do a ghost story. It takes place in this old mansion that looks a lot like Marygrove. Down in the basement."

"But of course. Marygrove is the perfect place for a ghost story. So what happens?"

"I'll let you know."

Enid grinned. "When you figure it out."

Crunch grinned too. "Yeah, when I figure it out."


After the conference he headed for the gym. If the day camp wasn't using it, the guys planned to shoot some baskets. One-handed basket shooting was not something he'd tried yet. He hoped he wouldn't lose his balance, fall over, and break the other arm. But if he'd managed some

32

one-armed tennis, he guessed he could manage some one-armed basketball.

James and Stu were waiting for him inside. "Danny isn't coming," Stu announced. "He says he has to spend the afternoon writing."

James struck his hand against his head. "My God, he's taking this place seriously."

"I can't write during the day anyway," Stu said. "Only at night."

"I can't write day or night," James retorted. "I have better things to do."

"Especially at night," Crunch commented.

"Just like you," James returned.

"Not yet," Crunch said.

"That's because you can't seem to make up your mind," Stu said. He tossed the ball to Crunch.

Crunch managed to snag it with his good hand. "Listen," he said as he lobbed it toward James, "I'm here because I'm a cripple. Why the hell are you here?"

"I'm a cripple too," James said. "A different kind of cripple." He dribbled the ball toward the basket, and then, with an easy lay-up shot, dropped it through.

"I've got to get into the basement of Marygrove," Crunch said. "If I'm going to set a ghost story in that place, I've got to know what it looks like. How am I going to do it? Got any ideas, Stu?"

Neatly, Stu nabbed the rebounding ball. "Other than asking Dobkin for the key, which he won't give you? No."

"We could break in," James suggested.

"If it comes to that, I'll call on you," Crunch said.

\*　　\*　　\*

33

An authors' agent, Dorothy Mannheim, came for dinner. Afterward, they pulled a couple of tables together and sat around pelting her with questions.

"Did you ever hear of a kid our age getting published?" Danny wondered.

"Lately several novels by young people still in college have made quite a stir," Dorothy replied. "But I think the best outlets for high school students are contests run by magazines such as *Seventeen* and *Scholastic*."

"If one of us sent you something," Sierra queried, "would you read it? I mean, even though we're just kids?"

Dorothy turned to Enid, a kind of desperation in her glance. "You're putting Dorothy on the spot," Enid said. "She's a very busy woman."

"Of course, I'm always looking for new talent," Dorothy added. "But I think you should wait awhile, develop a little, before you try to publish."

"When you read a manuscript by a new writer," Eve asked, "what are you looking for?"

"Something salable, of course," Dorothy said. "I have to make a living, and so do the writers for whom I work. But I want to tell you something. It's never salable unless it's written with some kind of conviction. The worst junk on the best-seller list was written by someone who on some level believed in it. If it doesn't have that kind of conviction behind it, it's usually not readable. It lies on the page like stone."

"But sometimes," Crunch said, "a person can pour out his whole heart, and it can be boring as all hell." He was thinking of Martina, whose turgid prose seemed to collapse under the weight of her adolescent agony. And

34

Rhonda—well, her stuff wasn't boring, exactly, just confusing. Today she'd written about an abandoned child. "You?" Crunch had asked, even though he suspected the question was perhaps too personal.

"None of your business," she'd returned sharply.

Enid had supported her. "Whether the subject of Rhonda's piece is herself or not is entirely irrelevant," she'd said.

But now Enid was agreeing with Crunch. "You're right. If you can't give your pain some shape, something that other people can connect to, it makes very dull reading. However, Dorothy was talking about published authors. Almost all of them write as well as they can. That's hard to believe sometimes, but I think it's true."

"I'll make a bargain with you," Dorothy said. "When you think you're ready, when you really think that, send me what you've done. Mention in the cover letter that you met me at Hudson Manor in 1988, and I promise you I'll read it. You'll know best when the right time has come."

Sierra raised her hand. "Yes," Dorothy said, resignation in her voice.

"I'm ready," Sierra replied. "I'm ready now."

Holding his stomach, James leaned over the table as if he were about to throw up.

"Sierra, how can you be so sure?" Kent asked.

"Audrey Gossett told me the short story I did for her last year is definitely publishable. You've heard of Audrey Gossett, of course."

"I can't say that I have," Dorothy returned mildly.

"I'm surprised. She's a very famous writer. Last year

35

she taught a creative writing course at Sand Hill. That's my school," Sierra added, in a tone suggesting that anyone who hadn't heard of Audrey Gossett could not be expected to know much.

"Boy," Rhonda said. "Audrey Gossett taught you? That's really fantastic. You're so lucky. Audrey Gossett, I can hardly believe it."

It seemed to Crunch that Rhonda was being sarcastic. Sierra, however, took the remark at face value. "Well, Rhonda," she said, "I'm glad at least someone around here has some education."

"Perhaps I could look at your story," Enid suggested.

"Oh, I don't have it here," Sierra said. "I couldn't possibly bring *everything* I've written with me."

"Send it to me," Dorothy said. She seemed to sense there was no other way to end the exchange. "Remember to mention this conference in your letter."

"Oh, you'll remember me," Sierra retorted. "Who could forget a name like Sierra McCaughey?"

She made it up, Crunch thought. She made up her name. He would find out her real name. He hoped it was something like Gertie Glitch. Somehow he would find it out, and from then on that's what he would call her. Gertie Glitch. He and everyone else at the conference. Gertie Glitch. Gertie Glitch.

"Gertie Glitch," Crunch said later, when a bunch of them were sitting around in the dorm lounge watching late-night TV. Well, not watching, actually. The TV was on, but they were mostly talking and wolfing down pizza for which they'd sent out. Having eaten scarcely any dinner, they were always hungry at night, but this eve-

36

ning they'd spent so long talking to Dorothy Mannheim, they'd decided to skip the trip into town.

"Who's Gertie Glitch?" Didi asked.

"A ghost. The main ghost in my ghost story."

"Of which you haven't written a line," Beth said.

"It's only Tuesday," he retorted. "The first Tuesday."

Beth glanced at her watch. "It's Wednesday."

Arms entwined, Meg and James wandered into the lounge. "Christ, I'm hungry," Meg said. "Afterwards, I'm always hungry."

Eve gazed at the two of them for a long moment. Crunch watched her face. Was she jealous? he wondered. Judgmental? Or merely curious? He couldn't tell. She shoved the last remaining pie in their direction. "It's cold," she said, "but if you're really hungry, I guess that won't matter."

"Too bad we can't get into Queen Bea's kitchen and reheat it," James said.

"That's all you have to do—wake them," Rhonda warned. "They'll send us all to bed, like we were seven years old."

"They can try," James responded grimly.

"I can't figure them," Danny said. "Everyone else here treats us like equals. They're the only ones who've come down with all these rules. I mean, when are we supposed to get our writing done, if we have to have our lights out by one A.M.? They don't understand what this conference is all about."

James clapped his hand on Danny's shoulder. "I'll tell you something, buddy. Neither do I."

"Then what did you come for?" Danny asked.

"Same as Crunch. Nothing better to do."

37

"Why didn't you go to a painting camp?" Eve queried gently. "You draw so well."

"If he were at a painting camp," Meg said, "he'd be writing."

James grinned. "That's right, babe."

Meg waved a hunk of pizza in his face. "Don't you 'babe' me," she warned.

"Any pizza left?" Linda asked as she entered the lounge.

Stu rose to his feet. "Sure," he said. "I saved some for you." He picked up the white cardboard box and carried it over to her, engaging her for several moments in conversation it was not possible to overhear. After she'd eaten, she spoke briefly to Didi, and then, hand in hand, she and Stu left the room.

Didi perched on the arm of Crunch's chair. "You want to get out of here?" she asked. "Go for a walk? Like Linda and Stu?"

Stu had achieved the goal he'd been working toward since supper Sunday night on the veranda of Marygrove. He was alone with Linda. He was committed for the duration.

Crunch, however, wasn't ready to do the same with Didi and permanently cross unwilling Eve off his list. On the other hand, taking a walk was not the same thing as signing a contract. In a four-guy, eight-girl situation, it was only chivalrous of the guys to spread themselves around. "Okay," he agreed.

"Good," Eve thought as she watched Crunch and Didi leave. "He's settled on her. Now he'll get off my back." He was really the only person at Hudson Manor she couldn't stand. Well, Sierra too, of course. But she knew why she didn't like Sierra. Sierra was obnoxious. Crunch was not. At least no one else seemed to think so. Eve didn't know why she found Crunch so annoying. With the good looks and easy-going style of the hero of teen movies, he was the kind of kid who was automatically popular wherever he went.

Eve, Rhonda, and Beth were sitting on the floor near the soda machine. Danny dropped three quarters in the slot, retrieved his diet Sprite from the machine's maw, and dropped down next to them. "I don't know anyone who goes to Maimonides Hebrew Day," he said to Eve. "Tell me about it."

"It's just a school," she replied. "Like any other school."

"It's a Jewish school."

"Yeah. Like New York Collegiate is a WASP school."

"I go to Collegiate, and I'm a Jew."

"Okay. Collegiate is for smart, rich New York Jews who want to look like WASPs. Maimonides is for smart, rich New York Jews who want to look like Jews."

"You got it," he said with a laugh. He held out the soda can, offering her a sip. She shook her head. "But you're here," he added.

"Obviously."

"I mean, the food's not kosher, and we're supposed to drive into Manhattan for a matinee Saturday."

"I told you, I'm not kosher. Neither is my mother. Since she's married my father, she's kept a kosher home, but she's still not what you'd call observant. I'm more like her in that respect."

"So it's he who wants you to go to a Jewish school," Rhonda commented.

"I don't mind," Eve said. "I'm glad I know Hebrew well, and that I study the Bible and the Talmud. All that stuff's really interesting, and important too, I think. You can be Jewish and care about Jewish culture without being religious."

"Don't you believe in God?" Beth queried.

Trust Beth to turn a conversation heavy at the first opportunity. Eve seized the question as if it were a spear and shot it back at her. "Do you?"

"Sometimes. Now and then." Beth turned to Danny. "How about you?"

"I'm an existentialist."

"You can be an existentialist and believe in God. Like Kierkegaard."

"Or A. J. Heschel," Eve said.

"I don't believe in God," Danny said. "I hope in God."

"I believe in praying." Rhonda had removed her beret and was rolling it up into a narrow tube. "I think if you pray long enough and hard enough, *someone* will hear you. It doesn't hurt to write a letter now and then, either."

"To God?" Eve asked.

Rhonda smiled but did not reply. "You still haven't answered Beth's question," she said.

"I don't believe in God," Eve returned firmly. "After Hashoah, how could I?"

" 'Hashoah'?" Beth asked. "What's that?"

"Hashoah's the Hebrew word," Danny said. "For the Holocaust."

Eve felt herself flush painfully as she always did when she had to explain the Holocaust to someone who wasn't Jewish. But she also felt such explanations were her duty. "When the Nazis cooked six million Jews in ovens," she said, her hands folded tight in her lap, as if to prevent the discomfort she was feeling from revealing itself in her face or her voice. "Six million Jews and four million other people—give or take a million here or there."

"I met your father once," Danny said.

"Really?"

"I didn't actually meet him. He spoke about the Holocaust at our school last year. He was terrific."

"He's a marvelous speaker. He knows what he's talking about. No shouting, no dramatics, no horror stories, but when he's through, your heart is in your mouth."

Danny nodded agreement. "Since your father is the one who wants you to go to Maimonides," he said, "does that mean he believes in God?"

"My father is a very stubborn man. But I'm not sure if he believes in God or not. We've never discussed it. Sometimes I think he goes to synagogue for the same reasons I don't eat pork. It's a way of saying, 'See, Hitler? This Jew is alive, and you're dead.' " She reached out her hand. "You know, Danny, I think I could use some of that soda after all."

He handed her the can. She took a long, slow sip and then returned it to him. "Thanks. Well, there's nothing I'd like more than to sit here talking about God and all that other good stuff with you guys, but I'm exhausted. I'm going to bed." She stood up. "Good night. See you in the morning."

She left the room. Some of the others saw her go, and their good-nights, like Danny's and Beth's, trailed after her.

But once in her room, with the door shut, she couldn't go to sleep. After that conversation she knew she'd dream again, and she didn't want to do that. She'd sit up for a while making notes about what she wanted to do for her major project. She thought she'd like to try something funny. Something totally absurd. Something with a very happy ending.

# First Wednesday

"There's talent in this room," Enid said. "A lot of talent. But something's missing. I've been talking with you about your plans for your major project, and it seems to me that you're all afraid. Do you know what I mean?"

"I'm not afraid of anybody," James said.

"Only yourself," Meg commented. "Like the rest of us."

"That's exactly the point!" Enid exclaimed. "Thank you, Meg."

"You're welcome, I'm sure."

Enid ran her long, bony fingers through her hair. "You're not willing to dig down deep inside, bring up the real stuff. Maybe because that hurts too much. But you haven't a prayer of writing anything that's any good unless you do."

"Hey," Crunch exclaimed, "I'm doing a ghost story."

He felt betrayed, even though so far he hadn't written a line. He'd even dropped the one thing he'd decided on, the ghost's name, Gertie Glitch. He wanted it to be a real ghost story, not a silly one. "You said a ghost story was okay."

"I'm with Crunch," Danny commented. "I'm not into confession. My psyche is boring as all hell."

"Funny you should say that," Kent returned. "Because I think what you're doing is closer to what Enid's talking about than anything anyone else has tried."

He glanced at Enid, who nodded her agreement. "Danny is making a longish short story out of a number of brief pieces he wrote at school last year. Sort of a grown-up version of 'What I Did on My Summer Vacation.' "

"But that sounds like autobiography," Eve said. "Is that what you want from us, autobiography? If it is, I'm leaving now."

"No, it isn't my autobiography," Danny explained. "It's funny. At least I hope it's funny. I mean obviously the main guy resembles me, but it doesn't talk about what's going on in his head, his thoughts or feelings. It's about these crazy things that happen to him, what he sees, what he does."

"But you care about what this guy sees and does," Enid said. "Your work has some power. In some sense it must be autobiographical. I think anything you write that's any good is autobiographical. Maybe not recognizably so. But the emotions have to be emotions you've felt and understood if your piece is to have any validity." She turned to Stu. "Now you're writing this outlaw adventure, full of blood and guts. Fine. But even if you're describing events that could never happen to you or to anyone else, the emotions have to be real, and the characters have to be real. They may be purple pods from Uranus, but the reader has to be able to connect with them."

"You don't believe in Albrecht, do you?" Stu remarked mournfully.

"No," Enid replied. "*Make* me believe in him." She smiled as if she'd just offered him a dish of ice cream. "Well, we'll talk more about this in our individual conferences. For now, let's get on with today's exercise. We'll begin with an improvisation. You won't have time to think too much. Let's see where that gets us."

She took a quarter out of her jeans pocket and dropped it in Eve's lap. "You've got it," she said. "You don't want to part with it. And you, Rhonda, you want it. What happens now?"

Rhonda rose from her seat and walked toward her. "Hi, Ma," she said in a little girl's voice. "I need some money for school."

Eve's fingers curled tightly around the coin. "I can't give it to you. I only have a quarter."

"That's just what I need, one quarter."

"If I give it to you, I won't have anything left," Eve replied mournfully. "We'll starve."

"A quarter won't save us from starvation, so you might as well let me take it to school." Rhonda knelt at Eve's side. "See, a quarter isn't worth anything to you. I can get a whole lunch with it, at school. One day that I won't be hungry. In the meantime, Ma, you'd better apply for welfare."

Crunch smiled. So did most of the others. Eve stared at Rhonda. "I'm not your mother," she cried dramatically.

That's good, Crunch thought. That's a surprise.

45

Rhonda responded immediately. "I know that. I've always known that."

"You have?" Eve sounded startled.

"Of course."

"Then you understand." Eve crossed her hands over her heart. "If I were your real mother, I'd give it to you. Of course I'd give it to you. If I were your real mother, I'd give you anything. But I'm not your real mother, so I don't have to give it to you. And if you were my real daughter you'd never ask me for it."

"I wouldn't?"

"My last quarter? Of course not."

"You've got it backwards," Rhonda said. "I'm going to write my real mother a letter. I know she'd give me her last quarter."

"Yeah?" Eve snorted. "Where's she been all these years?"

Enid raised her hand. "Okay, that was a good beginning." Crunch was sorry. He wanted to know what answer Rhonda would have given to Eve's question. But Enid had other plans. "Now what I want you to do is take it from where Eve said 'I'm not your real mother' and write the rest of the scene the way you think it would play."

Crunch strolled out into the hall and sat in a window seat. A few of the exercises had stimulated him; this one did not. He managed to grind out a few lines. This took about seven minutes. Then he rose from his seat and strolled down the hall, looking into each classroom that he passed. If he found Stu, they could play trash-can basketball until it was time to go back into the resource center.

It was Eve he found first. She was seated at the teacher's desk, her head bent over her notebook. He slipped into the room so quietly she never lifted her face. For a

46

long moment he watched her scribble away at a furious pace. With effort he controlled the impulse to reach out his hand and touch the cloud of soft black curls that covered her head.

At last she came up for air. "Hey, what are you doing here?"

Crunch seated himself in front of her. "Listen, Teach, let's trade moms."

"What are you talking about?"

"Are you adopted?"

"No."

"Your mother is your real honest-to-goodness birth mother?"

"Yes."

"And she gives you whatever you ask for?"

"You missed the point. I don't ask."

"What are you, some kind of saint?"

She slapped her pen down on the desk. "Don't be absurd. My parents are different, that's all. Different from other people's parents."

"Well, naturally. Everyone's different. I bet Rhonda's are different too. Real different."

She stared him right in the eye. "Look, Crunch, I don't want to explain my family to anyone, least of all to you."

"Why do you hate me, Eve? I like you."

"You don't like me. You're just intrigued because you can't have me. That's not the same thing at all. If I fluttered around you like some of the others, you'd have had enough of me in a day and a half."

"That soon, huh?"

"Everything goes faster here. Because we're with each other day and night, and there's no one else. Look at Stu and Linda. They got together in two days, and it seemed like a long courtship. At home it would have taken a couple of months. But you see, the actual time together is the same."

"What do you mean?"

"We're sleeping between six and eight hours a night, let's say. So we've got, say, seventeen-hour days. If you're at school or working, and you have a girlfriend you don't live with, you see her maybe ten hours a week, max? Well, here you see her sixteen hours a day. A day equals a week and a half!"

"You've known me eight weeks, and you still hate me. Damn it, Eve, I'm just not that bad!" His words forced an unwilling smile to her lips. He pressed his advantage. "You don't have to go out with me. Just be a friend, that's all."

"Everyone's your friend, Crunch? Everyone?"

"Well, of course not. But I'm not paranoid. I think the best of people unless they do something to change my mind. Innocent until proven guilty. A basic American principle."

"I was born in France. We didn't move to New York full-time until I was ready for school."

"Are you trying to tell me you're not an American?"

"Well, we're citizens now. But my parents still have apartments in Paris and Jerusalem. My dad does a lot of traveling researching his books."

Paris. Jerusalem. New York. Was that supposed to explain something? But her remark about her father triggered an image in his brain. "Listen," he said, "I saw this guy interviewed on TV last year. He'd won some kind of big prize. Micah Streitman. Is he related to you?"

48

She nodded slowly. "He's my father. The prize was a Pulitzer. For history."

"He looked more like your grandfather."

"He married late. And he's had a hard life." She stood up. "I don't hate you, Crunch. You're okay. You're fine. Now, let me finish what I was doing."

"All right, Eve, forget it." He didn't need to bang his head against a stone wall. "I'll see you around."

In the middle of the afternoon the heat settled on the campus in impenetrable layers. Restless, Crunch couldn't nap. It was too hot to play basketball or tennis. On weekdays the pool was the exclusive property of the day camp. But maybe talking to someone would take his mind off the weather. He left his room, to find the lounge empty. Outside, under a huge oak in the middle of the lawn, he discovered James, Meg, and Beth, engrossed in one of their skinhead conversations. Eve sat a little to their left, her head leaning against the trunk, her eyes shut. Crunch plopped himself down next to Beth.

"Well, of course, I'm not going to leave," James was saying. He squeezed Meg's hand. "Not now that I've got you. But I'm not going to give in to those fascists either. I'm not going to write anything. What can they do about it?"

"Oh, come on, James," Beth protested. "Enid's no fascist."

"She's a phony hippie," James said. "Not a real one."

"There are no real hippies anymore," Meg said. "We're all phonies. Every one of us in one way or another. Even the real hippies were phony."

Crunch held up his hand. "I refuse to accept that. I'm

49

not a phony. There isn't a phony thing about me. What you see is what you get."

"Either a phony or shallow as a baby's bath," Meg amended.

"Sticks and stones may break my bones," Crunch returned, "but similes will never hurt me."

Meg laughed. "Not bad, man. Not bad. Maybe I'll have to take it back."

Eve opened her eyes. So she had been listening. "What do you mean, Meg? Why do you call us all phonies?"

"We none of us live what we believe. Not even James. If he did, he wouldn't be here."

"I'm only seventeen," James said. "I don't have total control over my own life."

"You would if you had the guts to go out and support yourself. But you see, you need to be comfortable in your rebellion. So what kind of rebellion is that?"

"No one lives according to what they believe," Beth said.

"Or almost no one," Eve amended. "A few saints, a few fanatics. I can do without them."

Beth nodded. "We make compromises to live. That's not being phony. Not so long as you know what you're doing. You have to make compromises. You're not alone in this world. You have to live with other people."

"Enid keeps telling us to write the truth. Pull the emotion up out of our guts, she says. That's what makes authenticity." Meg snorted. "Now Rhonda is certainly pulling her stuff up out of her gut. Some big secret about her mother. She hints at it in every single piece she writes, so it's got to be something real, and something she really wants people to know about, too. But so what?

50

Trying to make sense out of her work is like trying to find your way in the fog. It's not worth the effort."

Crunch lay back with his hands clasped beneath his head. "I think what Rhonda writes is sort of interesting. I'm sort of looking forward to her big piece." Eve's too, he would have added, if she hadn't been with them. "I'm going to write a mystery. To make it real enough for Enid, maybe I ought to sleep down there."

"Down where?" Beth asked.

"In the cellar of Marygrove. That ought to scare me good. And then I'll know how it feels. So then my story will be . . . authentic."

"You want company?" James asked.

"I'd like it," Crunch said. "I'd like company a lot. But if I'm not alone, will I be scared?"

"You can be scared," Eve said, "and the other person can be scared too. You don't have to be alone to be scared."

"You want to come along, Eve?" Crunch asked.

"No," she shot back. "Absolutely not. I don't read horror stories, I don't go to see horror movies, I hate being scared more than anything in the world."

"Okay, okay. I just asked."

"When are you going to do it?" James asked.

"First," Crunch said, "I have to find a way to get in. Better give me a day or so to figure that out."

"What about Randy Rory and Queen Bea?"

"I've also got to solve that one. At least they don't do bed checks, like at camp."

"I'm ready," James said, "whenever you are."

"Maybe Stu will come too," Crunch suggested.

"You're like a bunch of little boys, planning to spend the night in the haunted house," Meg commented drily.

"Exactly," Crunch agreed.

"Actually, that's fine," Beth said. "Kent says writing is play. Serious play. When kids play, they're very serious."

"Enid says fiction is a dream," Eve interjected quietly.

"It doesn't have to be just one thing," Crunch said.

For the first time Eve met his eyes directly. "That's probably the smartest thing you've said since you got here."

"And that," Crunch returned with considerable satisfaction, "is certainly the nicest thing you've said to me since *you* got here."

# First Thursday

It was Rhonda's turn to present and analyze one of her favorite literary passages. Her choice was odd, Crunch thought—a children's book, *The Little Princess* by Frances Hodgson Burnett. As if dressing to match, her hat today was a sprigged sunbonnet.

"I loved that book when I was a little girl!" Beth exclaimed. "I thought it was about me."

"Orphans are popular characters in children's books," Enid said. "That's because lots of kids imagine the insensitive clods they live with can't possibly be their real mother and father."

"I loved the book too," Linda said. "But I really am adopted."

"So am I," Rhonda admitted.

"Lots of people are adopted," Crunch said. In his head he was trying to put together all of Rhonda's mysterious little remarks. "You keep suggesting something more."

"Rhonda doesn't have to tell us anything she doesn't want to tell us," Eve interjected sharply.

Meg fixed her wide, pale eyes on Rhonda. "I think you do want to," she said. "You've dropped too many hints not to want to."

A gust of wind rattled the blinds Kent had drawn against the morning sun. Crunch didn't normally notice such a small sound, but in the otherwise perfect silence of the room it was as audible as a thunderclap. At last Rhonda spoke. "I have very good reason to believe," she said quietly, "that my birth mother is Audrey Gossett."

Sierra leaped to her feet. "Do you mean the writer?"

"Yes," Rhonda said. "The one you talked about. If I have any talent, I guess that's where it came from. My adoptive parents can barely fill up one picture postcard between the two of them."

Sierra sat down again and pulled her chair closer to Rhonda's. "But how do you know?"

"Mine was a private adoption, through a doctor," Rhonda explained, "when my parents lived in Palo Alto. They've been very cooperative in my efforts to locate my birth mother—the doctor less so, I'm afraid. But we've managed to narrow it down to three possibilities—one of them is Audrey Gossett. I wrote to all three of them just before I came here, but so far I haven't gotten any answers."

"Getting a letter like yours would be sort of a shock," Linda said.

"To say the least," Stu muttered.

"It's going to make some story," Danny said.

"If I want to write it," Rhonda replied.

"Look," Sierra said, "I know Audrey Gossett, and I live near her. If you hear from her, let me know. I can be sort of an intermediary for you." She rubbed her hands together. "My God, this is exciting. Audrey Gossett—wow!"

"Enid, do you know Audrey Gossett?" Didi asked.

"I can't say that I do," Enid replied.

"Do you know her work?" Crunch added.

"I can't say that I do," Enid repeated. "Now I certainly have good reason to look it up." She glanced at her watch. "But do you think we could get on with our discussion of the passage? We're running late."

"Rhonda tells us what she just told us, and you want to talk about writing?" Martina sounded indignant.

"That's what we're here for," Enid returned mildly.

"It's all right, Martina," Rhonda said. "Really, it is. It's no big deal. Lots of adopted kids today go looking for their birth parents."

"But their birth mothers aren't usually someone famous," Sierra said.

"I'm not sure," Rhonda reminded her. "Remember, I'm not sure."

"Well, now," Kent interrupted, "let's talk about the way Burnett handles Sara Crewe's loss of her father in *The Little Princess*."

Crunch barely listened to the conversation that followed. Literary analysis bored him anyway. He watched Sierra, who was hanging on Rhonda's every word. Once in a while Rhonda rewarded her with a smile. Gertie Glitch— he'd wanted to revenge himself on smarmy Sierra by christening her Gertie Glitch. Maybe Rhonda's revenge was even better. But of course Rhonda might be telling the truth. That was a possibility.

Later that afternoon Crunch and Stu stood behind the rhododendrons at Marygrove staring at the padlock and chain on the cellar door. Their efforts to soft-soap Dobkin into parting with the key had proved fruitless. "I've worked here thirteen years," he'd said. "You can't pull a trick someone hasn't tried before. The only one who can get a key off me is the headmaster. He has to come himself. He can't send no delegate."

Crunch knelt down and fingered the chain. "It would be easy to saw that through. It's half-rusted already."

"Even so, it would take time," Stu said. "Someone might see us or hear us. I don't want to do it anyway. It seems—well, too destructive somehow."

"We'll go to the hardware store in town and buy a new chain, and a new lock. This door will be better secured when we're done than it is now."

"But what about the key to the new lock? We just going to walk up and hand it to old Dobbie?"

"We'll send it to him in an envelope—anonymously. As for someone seeing us—it's not going to happen. Not if we work in the middle of the night. I think we could do it at high noon behind all these rhododendron bushes and still not be seen. And what if someone does catch us? So what'll they do to us? Throw us in jail?" He shook his head. "They'll just throw us out."

"I don't want to get thrown out," Stu protested. "I go to school here. Remember?"

"Then I'll get James. He'll help me."

"For sure."

"You just see if you can lay your hands on a file. Luckily I brought along a good flashlight."

"All right," Stu said. "I'll get you the file. Gus'll lend me one. Old Dobbie does most of the cleaning, Gus does most of the fixing. I'll tell him I need it for . . . for what?"

"You can't figure out a reason for needing a file? Albrecht the Outlaw would be ashamed of you."

"All right," Stu agreed. "I'll think of something."

"I'm going to the hardware store right now, to buy a lock and chain."

"I thought of something. Buy a file too."

"I'm not like you, Stu. I've got no source of income this summer other than my parents' generosity, which is not a thing you can rely on. I'll buy a file if I have to, but that'll be the end of pizza."

"Okay, okay, poverty I can understand. I'm on scholarship here all year round. I'll go look for Gus, like a good boy."

When they met again two hours later in Crunch's room, Stu pulled the file out of a paper bag and waved it aloft like a trophy. "I told Gus one of the legs on the metal bookcase in my room was shorter than the other. He said put a matchbook underneath it. I said suppose it fell on the head of some little freshman girl next year, and the school was sued for seven million dollars. So he said, 'Another thing I don't have time for.' So I said, 'I'll take care of it.' So he let me borrow the file." He plopped down on Crunch's bed. "What's this ghost story of yours going to be about, anyway? I mean, what's going to happen in the basement of Marygrove?"

"You know more about that than I do. I'm just hoping when I get down there I'll get an idea. So far I've been kind of stringing Enid and Kent along. I'm getting the hang of the exercises, though."

"Yeah. Some of yours aren't bad."

"Yours aren't either," Crunch returned. "At first I didn't like having to read them out loud. But it doesn't bother me anymore. After all, this isn't ninth-grade English at Lenape High School." Gently he ran his finger across the edge of the file. He'd be careful tonight when he sawed the padlock on the cellar door. And he'd make sure James was careful too.

Kent had rented the video of *Lilacs and Liverwurst* in preparation for Sylvie Hoving's visit on Monday. They sat in a lecture hall and watched it on a large-screen TV. It was after ten when they drifted out of Hudson Hall. "How about a walk along the river?" Didi suggested. "We can stop at Carvel on the way back. I'm sick of pizza." Immediately Danny, Rhonda, and Martina fell in with the plan. Then Sierra said she was coming too. Linda, Stu, Meg, Eve, and Beth quickly announced that they needed to work. Suddenly Danny changed his mind. "I guess I need to work too."

"Would you bring me back an ice cream sandwich?" Eve asked Martina. "I don't have any money on me. I'll pay you when you get back."

"Me too," Danny said. "I've got money." He reached in his pocket and handed Martina a five-dollar bill.

"Thanks, Danny," Eve said. "I'll pay you as soon as I get to my room."

"Oh, forget it. My treat." Jovially he clapped his hand on her shoulder and strolled with her down the path. Danny, having lost out with Linda, was working hard on Eve. If she'd been an ordinary girl, Crunch knew he could beat out Danny with both arms in casts. But Eve wasn't an ordinary girl. She was much more responsive to Danny than she'd ever been to Crunch, something Crunch found barely believable.

Crunch knew he didn't have a lot of time. Rory and Bea locked the dorm doors at midnight. Back in his room he quickly shoved the file, the new padlock and chain, and his flashlight into a plastic shopping bag from the hardware store. He rapped briskly on James's door. The two of them quietly left the building and strode across campus. The night was warm, still, and dark. Beneath the huge old maples and oaks on the lawn that stretched between the dormitory and Marygrove, they could scarcely glimpse the stars. Scattered lights glimmered from the third and fourth floors of the mansion, but most of the faculty apartments, abandoned for the summer, were dark. A single shaded bulb over the main entrance did little to pierce the blackness.

Crunch squeezed between two rhododendron bushes and turned the light of his flashlight on the cellar door. "I'll hold this," he said. "You'll have to saw. I can't, because of my arm."

He'd been right about the chain. It was so rusty that James made rapid work of cutting through it. Rapid but noisy. "Can't you be quieter?" Crunch begged.

"Rub metal against metal?" James returned sharply. "How can anyone do that quietly? But don't worry. There's no one close enough to hear."

"And if we're caught, what's the worst that can happen?" Crunch heard echoing in his head the words he'd said earlier to Stu. "They'll throw us out, that's all." Only Crunch realized that he was no longer so anxious to be free of the Hudson Manor Writers' Conference. He knew now that he wanted to stay until the end. He wanted to find out what was going to happen.

59

"Okay!" James exclaimed suddenly. "I've got it!" The chain broke in two pieces. He grabbed one in each hand and waved them triumphantly in the air.

"Put them in the bag," Crunch said. "I'll get rid of them later. We don't want anyone finding them. We want it to look as if someone official replaced the chain and padlock."

James obeyed. Then he grabbed the handle of the cellar door and pulled. The door lifted with an agonizing, unexpected creak, even louder than the sound of the file against the chain. "Like the door to King Tut's tomb," Crunch said with a nervous laugh. "I bet this one hasn't been opened in four thousand years either."

James was down the steps in a moment. Shivering in spite of the thick warmth of the night, Crunch followed more slowly. Inside, his shivering did not cease. Here the heat and the sun of summer never penetrated. The chill cut to his bones, and the odor of dampness, at once sharp and musky, assailed his nostrils.

He played his light around the room they had entered. The floor beneath their feet was of hard-packed dirt. Someone, sometime, had whitewashed the brick walls, but that had been long ago, for streaks of black mold had turned them dark again. Crunch had no difficulty standing erect. The beamed ceiling was more than six feet high. The room was cavernous in size, and totally empty.

The rays of his flashlight dimly illuminated an arched opening on the opposite side of the room. James clutched Crunch's sleeve as they moved toward it. "I'm nearsighted," he explained. "I don't see too well in the dark."

Nearsighted and a little nervous, Crunch thought. But he himself wasn't sorry for the comfort of a human touch.

On the other side of the arch they found themselves in a long, wide corridor, which curved away beyond their vision. Rooms, some like vaults with more arched entrances, others shut off by rough wooden doors, revealed themselves as they inched down the hallway. "Maybe there's a light switch here somewhere," James offered hopefully.

Crunch played his flashlight on the ceiling. "No fixtures, at least none that I can see. When they wired the house, I guess they didn't bother with this part of the basement."

"They could have put in one little bulb someplace," James complained.

"Well, they had to wire the utility room, I guess. God knows where that is."

James's fingers were still curled tightly around Crunch's sleeve. "Suppose your flashlight goes out. Maybe we should have dropped bread crumbs, so we could find our way out again—you know, like Hansel and Gretel." His tone was not entirely jocular.

"Didn't the birds eat Hansel and Gretel's bread crumbs?" Crunch recalled.

"No birds here," James pointed out.

"Only rats. They like bread crumbs too." Crunch knew he was teasing James a little. "Listen, my flashlight isn't going to go out. I put in new batteries and a new bulb before we came."

Except for cobwebs and the ubiquitous mold, the corridor was empty. The vaulted areas, though, housed occasional dust-covered piles that seemed to have been stored there long ago and then forgotten—lumber, cut into boards of varying sizes; old broken-down school desks that had neither been repaired nor thrown away; an upended up-holstered sofa into which rodents of one form or another had made generous inroads; some tools, including a pickax and a shovel. "What do you think are in those cartons?" Crunch wondered as his light played over a heap of card-board boxes blotched and curled from dampness. "Give one of them a kick, why don't you?"

James stared at Crunch. "Me?" he queried blankly.

"You don't like it down here much, do you?" Crunch commented.

"Do you?" James returned.

"It's kind of interesting." And maybe the most interest-ing thing was James's reaction. Crunch had never ex-pected James, the fearless flouter of authority, to be scared.

James straightened his shoulders, turned, marched to the boxes, and punched one with his fist. The side col-lapsed. "Empty," he said. "Empty boxes."

"I wonder about the rooms," Crunch said. "The closed ones. Are they empty too?" He pushed against a door with his elbow, and then with the full force of both his good arm and the one in the cast, but it didn't budge. "Locked," he said. "I guess we could break in if we wanted to."

"What for?" James asked.

Crunch nodded. There seemed no point in doing dam-age. They tried other doors. They weren't all locked. One room was utterly empty. "All this storage space," James said. "You'd think they'd need it."

"The place is so huge. Stu says we can't even get to the parts they do use from here," Crunch explained.

James pushed against another door. It opened easily. The walls were lined with wooden racks, designed to hold bottles. But all the racks were empty. "A wine cellar!" he exclaimed. "But no wine. Too bad."

"Hundred-year-old wine?" Crunch wondered. "What would it be like?"

"Marvelous," James said. "Or else vinegar. We could only find out by tasting."

"Poison maybe," Crunch suggested.

James grinned. Now he almost ran down the corridor in his eagerness to reach the final door, the door in the wall that faced them at the end of the hall. A metal bar and hook revealed that it had once been padlocked, but the padlock was gone.

James shoved it with his shoulder. Crunch stood behind him as the door swung open slowly. The flashlight's beam barely pierced the gloom inside. But it was light enough. James uttered an exclamation that was almost a cry. "I knew it," Crunch said softly. "I knew there was something down here. I knew it."

"You go in," James said. He was shivering now. "You can tell me about it."

"What's the matter, James?"

"I have a little problem with death," he returned drily. "A sort of love-hate relationship. You know, like Sid Vicious."

Crunch didn't stop to find out what he was talking about. He entered the room. No, "room" was the wrong word. He entered the shrine.

The walls were covered in dark wood, some of the panels warped and pulled away from the wall because of the dampness. A once-handsome thick maroon carpet, now half-eaten by whatever creatures inhabited the cellar, covered the floor, which in this room, unlike most of the

63

others, had been paved with bricks. Against the far wall, on a stand of reddish wood, cherry perhaps, or mahogany, rested a large oblong box made of some kind of whitish stone, maybe granite or even marble. It was large enough to hold the body of a human being. Carved into the lid was the reclining figure of a man dressed in a frock coat and high collar, his legs covered by the stone replica of a blanket. On either side stood three-branched brass candelabra, tarnished now to blackness, but nearly as tall as Crunch himself. The walls were covered with framed photographs.

Crunch stepped forward and heard the sound of glass crackling beneath his feet. His light revealed pieces of glass scattered on the carpet in front of the stone coffin. He bent to examine them and recognized them as bits of a broken vase, for fragments of flowers, far too withered to identify, were scattered among them.

He shone his light on the life-size relief. Marble eyelids were closed over sightless eyes; pale, veinless hands were crossed over the waistcoated bosom. He glanced up at the large photograph on the wall directly above the stone box. It depicted a demure, half-smiling bride in a bustled wedding gown grasping the largest bouquet of roses Crunch had ever seen. Next to her stood the groom, a somewhat older man attempting to gaze at the camera with proper Victorian seriousness, but unable to disguise the delighted surprise in his eyes. Crunch recognized him. There was no missing that nose as large and sharp as an eagle's beak. The bridegroom and the man carved on top of the box were one and the same.

"It's Erastus Grove!" Crunch exclaimed. "I know it is." He played his light along the walls. All the photographs

64

featured the same man, at various ages, in various poses. There were several in which he and the demure young woman stood among large groups of girls, sometimes on the porch, sometimes on the lawn of a pristine Marygrove, as yet untainted by creeping ivy and smothering rhododendron. "See? Here he is with some of the first students at Hudson Manor. Her too. Mary Grove. Come on in, James. It isn't scary. It isn't scary at all. Just a little weird."

James appeared in the doorway. His eyes seemed fixed on his feet. "Do you think his body is in that sarcophagus?"

Crunch turned toward him. "What's a 'sarcophagus'?"

"That thing. A stone container. Inside it there'd be a wooden coffin, and inside that there'd be a body. The Greek and Roman exhibits at museums are full of them."

"Well, I knew it was some kind of coffin. You could hardly miss that. I don't know whether his body's in there or not. Stu told me Erastus Grove is supposed to be buried in the graveyard at Holy Innocents church." James uttered what sounded like a sigh of relief. "But," Crunch continued cheerfully, "Stu also said maybe he isn't. Mary Grove might have built this memorial to him right in her own house just to save herself a trip to his grave every day. On the other hand, so what if she actually buried him down here? The body decayed to bones long ago."

"Crazy!" James managed to glance at the box for a brief moment. He turned away, and then his eyes were drawn back to it. This time he let them linger.

"They were nuts about each other," Crunch explained. "Stu says her ghost haunts the place."

"What about his ghost?"

"His too, I guess."

65

"You think they know this bizarre room is here? I mean, the headmaster and the students and everybody else who has anything to do with Hudson Manor?"

Crunch shook his head. "Well, Stu doesn't know. He would have told me if he did." Crunch lay his flashlight down on the sarcophagus and moving toward James, seized his arm. "Come on, old buddy. Come on in. Even a Stephen King fan like me knows there's really no such thing as a ghost."

"Yeah," James said, "I know. So I'm acting dumb. Sometimes I can't help it." He stepped forward and stared at the recumbent model of Erastus Grove. "I guess you can write your ghost story now, without any trouble. You don't have to spend the night."

"Couldn't anyway," Crunch returned. "I still haven't figured a way in or out of that door Randy Rory locks at midnight. Also, I still don't have a plot."

"Steal one. From Stephen King."

"Or from someone." Crunch nodded, smiling. "You know what we'll do? We'll get the others to come down here tomorrow night. We won't tell them why or anything. We'll just surprise them. I'll bring candles for these holders. First we'll get everyone good and scared, and then we can sit here and tell ghost stories. Everyone knows a ghost story—from Boy Scout overnights or reruns of *Alfred Hitchcock Presents*."

"If you know one," James wondered, "why don't you stop fooling around and just write it?"

"Look who's talking."

"I could write something if I wanted to," James said. "I just don't feel like giving Enid or Kent the satisfaction."

"What would you write about?" Crunch asked. "How nervous you were down here at first?"

James shook his head. "Don't worry, man, this little indoor cemetery is yours. I'm not going to steal it."

"So let's get the whole gang to come down here too," Crunch insisted. "This place is full of juice. Something interesting will happen."

"All right," James agreed. "If nothing better to do comes up."

# First Friday

"Interesting, Eve." Enid laid the manuscript on her desk. "Very interesting."

"What does that mean?" Eve asked. " 'Interesting' is a word people use when they don't want to say 'lousy.' "

Enid raised her eyebrows. "That's not what *I* mean. You'd have to work very hard to write something lousy. Clear and forceful sentences come naturally to you. But sometimes I think you might be better off writing nonfiction than fiction."

"I don't want to write nonfiction."

"Why do you want to write fiction?"

"I just do. Does there have to be a reason?"

Enid leaned back in her chair. "It's at times like this that I still long for one of those cigarettes I haven't smoked in ten years."

Eve leaned forward. "Just spit it out, Enid. I can take it."

"Well, now, take this story about Elmer Klampett. It's supposed to be funny."

"Only it isn't?"

"Well, it is, now and then. The New York City Bureau of Flora and Fauna—that's pretty funny. But in spite of all the wild and crazy things that happen to Bureau Chief Elmer Klampett in the story, it's just not funny very often."

"I read it to Beth, Rhonda, and Martina. They laughed their heads off."

"First, they're your friends. Second, your voice and gestures when you read aloud count for a lot. But humorous writing has to be funny when read by a person to himself all alone in a silent room. It's the hardest stuff of all to write."

"Okay, forget funny. I'll add chases and overturned trucks and shoot-outs. I'll make it into a pure adventure story instead of a comedy adventure."

Enid sighed. "Do you think you could lend a little plot to Martina, and borrow a little personal agony?"

Eve stiffened. "What do you mean?"

"Eve, what do you know about the pigeon problem in New York City? More to the point, what do you care about the pigeon problem in New York City?"

"But this is comedy. This is a joke."

"Don't you know where comedy comes from? Real comedy? It comes from the same place as any other really good writing." Enid pointed to her belly. "Right here, from your gut."

Eve grasped the edge of the desk with both her hands. "Listen, Enid," she said, "I like Martina. But I don't like her writing. All this turgid stuff about this girl who suffers terribly because her mother and father don't understand her. They don't beat her, do they? So who the hell cares? It's nothing. It's not worth writing about."

"To Martina it is. But you're right. She's got to shape it—find a way to say it that doesn't sound like whining. Your problem is the opposite. You get the surfaces all right. It's the feeling that's missing."

"So I'll give it up."

"This story?"

"No. Writing."

"Whatever for?"

"If I can't do it, I'll give it up."

"You don't mean that, not for a minute." Enid banged her hand down on top of the manuscript. "I'm not telling you that you can't write. I'm not telling you that you have no talent. I'm just telling you that you're not all the way there yet. No one here is."

"Danny . . ." Eve murmured. "Meg."

"Not even them. You certainly have as much potential as either of them. I knew that as soon as I heard your first piece. Remember? The one about your room? The feeling that came through in that one—we've seen it in a couple of other exercises. Perhaps when you're writing on your own, you censor your feelings. In class, you don't have the time to do that."

Eve gathered up the papers on the desk. "I'll see what I can do."

Enid stood up. She was smiling. She was always smiling. But now a note of apology crept into her voice. "Don't get me wrong, Eve. The pigeon piece has many virtues. Even if you go on just as you've begun, it will be entirely acceptable. We'll be delighted to publish it in *The Hudson Manor Review*."

70

That meant nothing, and Eve knew it. Something by everyone at the conference would appear in the magazine. Except maybe James, but that was only because almost halfway through, he still hadn't written a word. At least not a word that anyone had seen.

"Perhaps we can include a couple of exercises too," Enid added. "Think about the ones you might like to submit."

"All right." Eve rose from her chair and headed for the door.

"See you later," Enid called out pleasantly.

Eve did not reply. In the hall, clutching her notebook, Martina waited. "Your turn for the slaughter," Eve said.

"She really tore you apart, huh?" Martina said.

"In a nice way, of course. She never stops smiling, even while she's strangling you."

"If you got it, I can imagine what she'll do to me. She doesn't like my style anyway."

"Nor mine, my dear, nor mine. Thank God for Kent." They were now meeting with Enid and Kent on alternate days. Kent was much more willing to take her work at face value. He commented on what she'd done without lecturing her on what he thought she *ought* to be doing.

"Kent doesn't like my style either," Martina replied mournfully.

Eve wished she could say "I do." But since she couldn't, she merely remarked, "Oh, well, it doesn't matter. The important thing is we're here, we're writing, we're having fun. It's each other that matters more than the teachers anyway."

Enid poked her head through the door. "Oh, there you are, Martina. I've been waiting for you. Come on in."

Martina lifted a hand in farewell. Eve left the building. Outside, a group of day campers were playing kickball. She sat down in the coolness of the shade of a maple tree to watch, soon as absorbed in the game as they were. Though only five or six years old, they were as serious about their game as the Mets in a down-to-the-wire pennant race.

"Penny for your thoughts." Startled, she turned to see Crunch drop to her side.

She was just annoyed enough to tell him. "I'm sick of Enid. 'Write what you feel. Write what you feel.' That's not very helpful, is it?"

He pulled a penny from his pocket and dropped it in her hand. "Thanks. That's the second time you've spoken to me as if I were a human being. I'm making progress."

She laughed. "You haven't bothered with me for two whole days. We can just be friends, like any other two kids here, now that you've finally settled down with Didi."

"Have I?"

"Haven't you?"

Crunch shrugged. "That remains to be seen."

"You like to keep all your options open, don't you?"

"Don't you? No one ever knows what you're feeling."

Eve pulled up a blade of grass and tapped his hand with it. "Now you sound like Enid. Just because you don't doesn't mean no one does."

"So who does?"

She shrugged.

"Have you got a boyfriend, Eve?"

She could no more imagine bringing a boy into her house than she could imagine performing on the high wire at the circus. He'd find the scrutiny unbearable, in spite

72

of the kindnesses with which it would be covered. "You're pushing it, Crunch," she warned. "Keep it up and we'll be right back where we started."

Crunch stretched out, elbow on the ground, head resting on his hand, and gazed at her. "Okay, I'll change the subject. What are you writing? For your big project, I mean. That isn't a secret, is it?"

"I'm writing a story about the Great Manhattan Pigeon Cleanup of 1992."

"Sounds pretty funny."

"I think it's a barrel of laughs. Enid thinks it's about as funny as Cream of Wheat."

"Can I read it?"

"Well, you'll hear it. We're all supposed to read our stuff out loud the last day."

"So you don't want my help. Okay, I can handle that. But I sure could use yours."

Eve found Crunch's admission both touching and surprising. "I'll be glad to read anything you've written," she offered.

"So far there's nothing written."

"You and James. But unlike him, at least you do the set exercises. And they're not bad."

Crunch sat up so that he could strike his forehead with the flat of his hand. "Wow. I may faint." She smiled but said nothing. "If you think Enid's giving you trouble," he continued, "can you imagine what she's doing to me? Kent too."

"So what do you want from me?"

"I'm asking everyone. I want to do a ghost story. I have the perfect setting, but I'm having trouble dreaming up a plot. I thought we could all meet tonight in the basement of Marygrove—that's the setting. I know you don't like scary stuff, but we'll all be there so it can't be *too* scary. We can tell ghost stories, like we used to do around the fire at summer camp. . . ."

"I never went to summer camp."

"Well, you know what I mean."

She didn't, not really, but she nodded as if she did. She wasn't about to tell Crunch, or anyone, that although she was fifteen and a half, this conference was the first time her parents had allowed her to spend two nights in a row away from home. She'd fought like a threatened tiger for the right to come, locking herself in her room without dinner for three nights in a row when her parents had refused permission. She'd been almost as startled at her own vehemence as they were. But as soon as her English teacher told the class about the conference, she knew she had to go. Not just for the writing—that was the least of it. She had to go because it was time to go.

Her mother sensed that and gave in first. "Suppose she gets into Harvard or Yale," she'd said. "If she does, we can't make her commute to a New York City college. This will be practice for that."

"College is two years away," her father retorted. "She's too young."

"At a place like Hudson Manor, she'll be well supervised," her mother replied. "And it's only twenty-five miles from New York. It'll be all right."

"You'll call every day?" Her father's consent was so half-hearted that she didn't realize until hours later, alone in her room, the enormity of her victory.

She *had* called her folks every day, usually when the other kids were not around to notice. Crunch, who was still talking, wasn't aware of that either. "I figure everyone knows a ghost story," he said. "If we sit around telling them, I'll get some ideas."

"So we're to write your story for you."

"Not really. I'll have to adapt what I hear. Cut and paste. Change it around. But the real reason we want to do it is because it'll be fun. We'll supply the food."

"Who's we?"

"Me and James."

"Have you ever been down in that basement?"

"Yeah. James and I went down last night. That's when we had the idea."

"What's it like down there?"

". . . Surprising."

If everyone was going, she wasn't going to stick out like a sore thumb by not going. "What time?" she asked.

"We'll wander over right after that book review guy is done talking to us. About ten or so, I'd say. We'd make it later, but we don't want Randy Rory and Queen Bea to call out the troops. We're probably not supposed to be down in that cellar. Anyway, we didn't ask permission."

"Okay," Eve said. "I'll be there."

Crunch stood up and held out his hand. She took it and he lifted her to her feet. Side by side, they strolled across campus, not separating until they reached the dorm.

"Let me see," Eve mouthed.

James tilted his sketch in her direction. The jaunty bow tie and plaid jacket belonged to their guest, the book reviewer Gregory Hyde, but the face was that of a drooling wolf with large, leering eyes.

Eve nodded her approval. Rory's epithet "randy" was

75

merely alliterative; it would more appropriately have been bestowed on Mr. Hyde, who, though at least sixty-five, had managed, in the course of the evening, to put his arm around or bump knees with every girl in the group.

He was funny, though. Eve had to admit that. He was telling a long and complicated story about an author who'd tried to seduce him into giving her book a rave notice. "It was a good book," he said. "At least I thought so. I'd have written nice things about it if she'd left me alone. But of course, under the circumstances, I couldn't touch it with a ten-foot pole. The reviewer who finally did take the assignment panned it unmercifully. Poor Millicent D'Alessio. Her problem was that she was ugly. Really ugly."

Sierra smiled and batted her long lashes. "You mean, if she'd been pretty, things would have turned out differently?"

"Oh, certainly," Mr. Hyde returned. "I can't resist pretty."

"We've noticed," Eve murmured, just loud enough for James on one side of her and Beth on the other to hear.

"But," he added sharply, "it doesn't matter how pretty if the book's no good."

Sierra tugged her tube top not up, but down. Now, even if Mr. Hyde had the eyesight of a mole, he couldn't miss what had been perfectly evident all along. "If I ever write a good book, can I show it to you?" she asked.

"Why wait for a book? Show me a short story. Show me *anything*." Mr. Hyde was practically salivating.

"Sierra's not ready for that," Enid interjected sharply. "Do go on, Gregory. Tell us about the run-in you had with Tama Janowitz."

Mr. Hyde told an even longer and even funnier story.

They asked him some questions, and then it was time for him to go. The instant he rose to his feet, Sierra was at his side, her hand on his arm, speaking to him rapidly and quietly.

Enid came forward and said something to both of them. Sierra shot Enid a furious glance. Mr. Hyde put his hand over Sierra's. Then Kent joined them. "Good night, kids. Thanks," Mr. Hyde called out.

Enid and Kent added their farewells. Sierra, looking like the cat that swallowed the cream, said nothing. The four of them left the room.

"They're going up to Kent's apartment for a drink," Rhonda said. "Like they always do when we have a guest."

"This is the first time a kid has gone along," Linda noted.

"She wants that old fart, she can have him," Meg commented derisively.

"They won't *do* anything," Martina said, eyes wide. "I mean, Enid and Kent won't let them."

"If I know our Sierra, she'll find a way. And make him pay too," Meg replied.

"Oh, Meg!" Martina cried.

Meg put her arm around Martina. "That's what I like about you, honey. You're such a darling child."

"At least Sierra'll be occupied for the rest of the evening," Eve said. "We won't have to put up with her."

"Was she invited?" Crunch asked.

"She heard us talking at dinner. We had to tell her," Linda explained apologetically.

"She may yet show up," Crunch warned.

"She said the whole thing sounded pretty dumb to her," Linda added.

"So maybe we're safe," Stu commented. "Though with Sierra you never know what she's saying for effect and what she really means."

"You coming, then?" Crunch asked.

"He's coming," Linda assured him.

Stu seized Linda's hand. "If I get canned, I get canned. There are other schools—like yours."

"Sure," Linda said. "You're going to go to prep school in Kansas. That's all you need."

"You won't get canned," James said. "Believe me, no one, no one at all, could possibly find us down there."

"James and I are going on ahead," Crunch said, "to set things up. You guys come over in half an hour. Stu will show you how to get in."

"Can I come with you?" Didi asked. "Can I help?"

Crunch regarded her steadily for a moment. Then he glanced at Eve. She turned to Beth. "I have to go back to the dorm to get my sweater," she said. "Wait for me, and I'll walk over with you."

Crunch returned his gaze to Didi. "Sure. Come on."

The three of them loped off.

Eve sat alone, near the door, watching. It was as far as she could get from the sarcophagus. She'd seen plenty of them in the Metropolitan Museum of Art, but she didn't like them. They were coffins, of course, but there was more to the discomfort they inspired in her than that, though she wasn't sure what.

The others were huddled together, in a circle, lit only by the flickering light from the candles burning in the candelabra and in the holders a few of them had had the foresight to bring along. She couldn't even see James's face, or Crunch's, for they'd deliberately pulled forward the hoods on their sweatshirts to shadow their features. James had told the first story, "Two Bottles of Relish." It hadn't scared her much when she'd read it, but hearing it told out loud, hollow-voiced, in this fantastical Victorian mausoleum, was quite another matter, and she found herself giggling nervously at the scariest parts, just like Didi and Rhonda and Martina and Linda, even though she knew perfectly well what was going to happen.

"That's it!" Crunch replied when James was finished. "That's my story. I'll write it down just as it is. That is, unless you want it, James."

"I wouldn't bother," James responded in his normal voice. "Lord Dunsany's already done it."

"Nuts!" Crunch exclaimed. "Doesn't anyone have a story that hasn't been written down someplace?"

But Danny told "Invasion of the Body Snatchers." He'd seen all three film versions four times each. Meg recounted a horror story by Lovecraft, and Didi delivered a shortened version of one of the Audrina novels by V. C. Andrews. Beth had arrived with a book in hand, from which she read a story called "A Rose for Emily." It wasn't horrifying until the end, but then it horrified them all quite enough, and amazed them too, when Beth revealed that it was by William Faulkner.

"I don't know any ghost stories," Martina said when Crunch tapped her on the shoulder with a long stick he was using like a bony finger. "I'm sorry, but I just don't."

"Have you ever been scared?" Rhonda asked.

"Well, of course," Martina replied.

"Tell us about that then," Rhonda suggested. "That'll be okay, won't it, Crunch?"

"Excellent," Crunch said. "Maybe even better."

Sure, Eve thought. Now he stands a chance of getting something he can use without Enid's screaming "Plagiarism!"

"It hardly matters what you say in this room," Linda said. "It'll all come out sounding scary."

For a moment no one spoke. The flashlights had been switched off; the only light came from flickering candles. The corners were dark and shadowy; the pictures on the wall mere shimmering splotches. Eleven dim forms huddled on the floor, their faces half-hidden in shadow. Only the pale stone coffin, with its ghastly statue carved on the lid, was vividly etched in the spectral light, drawing all eyes to it, willing or not.

Eve broke the silence. "What I'd like to know about this room," she said softly, "is the truth. Why did Mary Grove build this shrine to her husband?"

"Because she loved him," Stu said.

"Lots of wives love their husbands, and they don't do this when they die," Eve said.

"Everyone reacts differently," Didi said.

"That's just it," Eve agreed. "They do. The question is, why?"

"In this case, we'll never know," Crunch said. "All the people involved are long dead."

"Unless one of these panels is actually a secret door," Meg said. "And we open it. And behind it we find Mary Grove's private journal. . . ."

"And a bunch of love letters she and her husband wrote to each other," Beth chimed in.

"She and her husband?" Meg snorted derisively. "No! She and her lover. What was his name? Archibald, I think. Archibald MacGregor."

"Together, they murdered poor Erastus," Rhonda said.

80

"Of course," Stu agreed.

"Keep going, keep going!" Crunch cried. "How did they murder him? How?"

"They hired the outlaw Albrecht to do the actual job," Stu said. "He pretended to be a Latin teacher. . . ."

Meg, Beth, Stu, Rhonda, Danny, and James spun a story so wild that the eeriness of the room dissipated in gales of laughter. Crunch grabbed Beth's notebook and scribbled rapidly on blank pages as they spoke, a gleeful grin pasted on his face.

"You'd better change the names," Stu suggested. "I mean, there's a history of Hudson Manor in the library. I've never read it, but I bet the chapters about Mary and Erastus Grove are nothing like this."

"Sure I'll change the names," Crunch said. "Sure I will. I'll have to fix it up. Smooth it out and everything. But this is good. It's really good."

"We give it to you," Meg said with a wave of her hand. "We give it to you gladly, in exchange for an absolutely smashing evening. It's the least we can do."

Martina sighed. "It's so easy for you guys. How do you do it?"

"Martina," Eve said, "tell us your story. The one you were going to tell before you were so rudely interrupted."

"No," Martina said, "I have no story. That's what I said. I don't know any ghost stories."

"But then," Eve reminded her, "Rhonda asked you if you'd ever been scared, and you said yes, of course. So tell us."

Martina shook her head.

"Come on, Martina," Crunch said, "we're all taking a turn." He took her hand and squeezed it. "We're friends."

For a moment she stared into his face, drinking in the warmth and apparent guilelessness of his smile. When she spoke, her voice had dropped almost to a whisper. "The time I was most scared in my whole life had nothing to do with ghosts," she said. "Nothing to do with ghosts or graves or cemeteries, or anything like that. I was about seven. I woke up in the middle of the night because I heard my parents screaming at each other. They never screamed. They never even argued. I got out of bed and sat at the top of the stairs, shivering, even though it wasn't cold. I started to cry, and they heard me and they came and got me. They both hugged me and kissed me and told me everything would be all right."

"And was it?" Eve asked softly.

Martina shook her head. "I knew it wouldn't be. My father left two weeks later, and then they got a divorce. So I was right to be scared."

"But it *is* all right now," Crunch offered hopefully.

"You get over those things," Martina said. "Of course you get over them. But I can still remember exactly how I felt, sitting at the top of those stairs, shivering and sobbing. You don't forget either." She looked around the room. "That's no kind of a ghost story. It couldn't scare anyone else. But it scared me."

"I'll tell you the scariest thing that ever happened to me," James said. With a restless gesture he pushed back the hood of his sweatshirt, suddenly revealing his pale, naked face. "I thought I wanted to die. I washed thirty Valium down with a fifth of bourbon. Right before I passed out, I realized dying was the last thing I wanted to do. But I thought I was going to anyway. So I was scared."

His recital was almost tonelessly matter-of-fact. But for

a moment after he was done, the only sound in the room was the hissing of the candle flames. Then Meg said, "But you haven't stopped."

"Stopped what?" James asked.

"All that stuff."

"I guess I still think I want to die sometimes. But maybe I don't swallow so much stuff. Maybe I'm improving. Maybe that dumb shrink's doing me some good after all." He turned to Crunch. "Once you asked me what I was doing here."

Crunch nodded.

"The shrink thought it would be a good idea, and so did my mom. They bribed me—told me I could spend Christmas in Paris, where my dad lives, if I'd come. So I came—even though I knew it would be dumb."

"Are you sorry?" Meg asked. He merely smiled as she put her arm around his shoulder. They sat there silently as others spoke. But they were listening. They were all listening. It seemed as if Martina's confession had opened a floodgate. One by one they spoke their fears. Danny had been mugged in Central Park. Mountain climbing in Colorado, Linda had almost fallen from a teetering rock overhanging a chasm. Didi had watched while a car ran over and killed her friend. Stu's mother lived with leukemia. He was scared every day. A neighbor's pit bull had attacked Beth. She rolled up her cutoffs to show the five-inch scar on her thigh.

Gently Rhonda touched Beth's wounds. "How did this session turn into show-and-tell?" she wondered.

"What do you want to tell us, Rhonda?" Beth asked. Her usually dogmatic voice had sunk about an octave, acquiring an almost hypnotic quality.

Rhonda removed her khaki forage cap and placed it in her lap. "Sometimes I exaggerate. I kind of . . . make up stories."

"Everyone here does that," Stu pointed out.

"You're talking about writing. That's different. I make things up, well, you know, like I wear hats."

"To be noticed," Beth said.

Rhonda nodded. "If you look like me, you have to do something."

"Stories like you're adopted?" Crunch asked. "And Audrey Gossett is your mother?"

"Yeah," Rhonda said. "I mean, I am adopted. But I haven't set off on any search for my birth mother. She didn't want me, I don't want her. The parents I've got are as much as I can handle."

"You telling the truth now?" Meg asked.

"You'll never trust me after this, will you?" She sighed. "Well, it's what I deserve."

"You don't need to lie," Martina said.

"They're not lies," Rhonda replied defensively. "They're stories."

"All right, stories. You don't need to tell stories. Everyone likes you anyway. You're fun." There was more than a touch of envy in Martina's tone.

"Do you think," Crunch wondered, "that one reason you made up the Audrey Gossett story was sort of to get Sierra?"

Rhonda nodded. "For sure. That's not very admirable either."

"Oh, don't worry about it," James said. "It was a good trick."

Eve listened, half-admiring, half-appalled. How could

they reveal such intimate moments? And yet how wonderful for them that they could. She disliked the confessionals Martina composed, heavy with obscure symbolism and elaborate language, yet these stories tonight, told simply and directly, moved her.

Still, she could not tell her own. "You, Eve?" Crunch asked. "Have you ever been scared?"

"Of course I've been scared."

"So?"

She shook her head. She could have made something up, like Rhonda. But she would not demean what she took to be their truths by doing that. On the other hand, she would indulge in no self-pitying confessional either.

"You're not going to tell us?" Crunch asked.

"That's right," Eve said. "I'm not going to tell you."

"We all told you!" Crunch exclaimed.

"Leave her alone, Crunch," Beth insisted. "Eve has a right to her privacy, if that's what she wants. We're not nine years old, and this isn't a bull session at an overnight birthday party."

"Thanks, Beth." Eve turned and faced Crunch. "You've told us nothing either."

"I'm scared before every wrestling match," Crunch admitted quietly. "Most times, I actually throw up. But I do it out behind the school, where none of the guys can see me."

"It's all right to be scared before a big game," Stu said. "Everyone is."

"It's like being scared before you go on stage in a play," Rhonda said. "It hardly counts, it's so normal."

"Maybe that's why you read ghost stories," Martina suggested. "To *really* scare yourself. I don't have to. I'm scared enough without them."

Beth glanced at her watch. "It's quarter of twelve," she announced. "Soon we all turn into pumpkins."

Crunch snuffed out the candles. For a moment the room was in utter blackness. Then he switched on his flashlight. They made their way out of the crypt and down the long, wide corridor. Crunch waited while they climbed the cracked and flaking cement steps. The last one out, he shut, chained, and padlocked the door.

Walking across campus, Eve listened to them teasing, laughing, shouting, as they always did. But she knew something was different. Something had happened to them down there. They had coalesced. They knew things about each other now, deep and private things. They liked her well enough. To them she was no Sierra. But when they were all giving, she, only she, had refrained. As usual, she was on the outside.

She remembered one August day long ago, sitting on the porch at the Cornicks' cottage on Cape Cod. Three of the four noisy girls who summered next door came barreling by on their bikes. "Hey, Eve," the middle one called. "Get your bike and come with us." Tires screeching, the three of them ground to a halt by the front gate.

"I don't have a bike," Eve said.

"You can borrow Rachel's," the youngest offered. "She went to Provincetown."

Her longing to go with them was so great that it made her head throb. But she had to turn them down. "I don't know how to ride a bike," she admitted.

"You don't?" Utter amazement was engraved on all three faces. "How come?"

Because my parents won't let me ride a bike, she thought. Because they believe bikes are dangerous. But she couldn't say that to the girls. She couldn't betray her parents in that way. They protected her because they thought she was fragile, breakable. She wasn't, but they were, and so in reality it was she who had to protect them. "No reason," she said. "I just never learned."

The girls rode off, leaving her alone. Alone, alone, always alone. Even when she wasn't alone, she was alone.

Like right now. But she couldn't help it. Some mistakes can't be rectified; some illnesses can't be cured. There are things about which nothing can be done. That's how it was, and that's how it would remain.

# First Saturday

Danny was the last one to climb into the van. Before he squeezed into the only remaining seat, he turned and grinned at the sight of the rest of them jammed together, chattering and laughing like little kids on a kindergarten field trip. "What a bunch!" he exclaimed. "You'd think we'd never been anywhere in our lives."

"You're as glad to leave the campus for a day as the rest of us," Crunch said, "even though you live in New York City."

"You're damn right," Danny replied. "The atmosphere had gotten a little hermetic.

"Hermetic?" Crunch didn't think he'd ever heard that word before.

"Sealed off," Danny explained. "Like your basement room."

Crunch shook his head and pointed to Kent in the driver's seat.

"Don't worry," Danny said, "there's too much racket in here. He can't hear a word any banana in this bunch is saying."

Bunch of bananas. That's what they'd become last night, Crunch thought—a bunch. Except for Sierra of course. And Eve. From Sierra he'd expected nothing, but he felt himself profoundly disturbed by Eve's behavior. It wasn't only he, Crunch Oliver, she was rejecting. Her refusal to speak the night before was a rejection of them all.

He realized, to his surprise, that he was actually angry with her. She was a knockout, her looks enhanced by her own apparent obliviousness to them. Nothing could change that. But beauty wasn't everything. Accessibility meant something too. Crunch made up his mind that he was through with her. Danny was seated next to her now, waving his hands around and laughing as he told her some long, elaborate story Crunch made no effort to overhear. She was laughing too. Good. Danny could have her. He was probably the only person at Hudson Manor she thought was good enough for her.

Crunch was sitting next to Didi. Stu and then Linda were on his other side. Linda's notebook was open on her lap, and she was reading aloud the assignments Enid had left them before going home for the weekend.

*Saturday*. While you're in New York City, record the best conversation you overhear between or among people you don't know.

*Sunday*. A man climbs out of a van, trips, looks around in embarrassment, and sees a woman smiling.

Describe the above event using the characters and

elements of setting in three completely different ways. You may do the exercise in the distinctive styles of three different authors, such as Hemingway, Henry James, William Carlos Williams, T. S. Eliot, Jack Kerouac, or any others you might choose. Or you may select varying genres or media. Make sure that you radically vary tone, sentence structure, voice, distance, point of view, and word choice in each sample.

"Listen," Stu said to Crunch, "let's you and me and Linda and Didi sit on the steps of the Metropolitan Museum of Art. All kinds of crazies show up there. We'll overhear plenty, for sure. Then afterward, we can ride down Fifth Avenue."

"Sounds fine to me," Crunch said. He turned to Didi. "Okay with you?"

"Oh, yes," she returned eagerly. "Just great."

Didi really liked him. He had no doubt about that. Though her obvious adoration could be a drag, right now he was enjoying it. He took her hand in his. With a contented sigh she squeezed it.

In the end, though, they stayed too long at the museum and had to take the subway instead of the bus downtown, arriving at the theater just in time for the matinee. Afterward they had dinner at a little restaurant Danny knew in Greenwich Village. As Crunch headed for the seat between Didi and Rhonda, Sierra pushed in front of him and grabbed it without apology or explanation. Annoyed, he sat down opposite Didi and glared at Sierra.

She ignored him. Rhonda had captured all her attention. "Kent told me the bookshops down here are open late," she said. "We can stop in one of them after dinner."

Rhonda drew back as if she'd just discovered Sierra had an infectious disease. "What for?"

"Don't you think it'd be a good idea to read something your mother wrote before you hear from her? I really think you should have done that even before you sent her a letter."

Rhonda turned away and glanced nervously across the table. "You'd better tell her," Crunch said.

Sierra frowned. "Tell me what?"

Rhonda bowed her head. Again, it was hard to know if her contrition was deeply felt or manufactured. "I made up that story. You know, the way we do."

Sierra's frown deepened. "Yeah?"

"I never heard of Audrey Gossett before you mentioned her. She's not my birth mother. I don't know who my birth mother is, and to tell you the truth, I don't care."

For a moment Sierra seemed struck dumb.

"I can't believe you don't care at all," Linda said.

"Not enough to go looking for her," Rhonda amended.

"What am I supposed to believe?" Sierra asked bitterly.

"What I just said," Rhonda replied. "It's the truth."

Slowly Sierra shook her head. "Why did you make up such a story?"

Rhonda shrugged. "For laughs, I guess."

Kent was sitting at the head of the table. Sierra stood up, picked up her chair, and carried it over to him. "Move over," she said. "I'd like to sit next to you."

Kent looked startled, but he made room. Poor Kent, Crunch thought. He was the only one in the room who absolutely had to be nice to Sierra.

After dinner they walked the streets of the Village and visited a couple of clubs, where they listened to music.

Meg and James were clearly together, like Stu and Linda. Eve and Danny were together too, but Rhonda and Beth were almost always with them. Crunch couldn't quite tell whether they were a couple or not. And then he told himself to stop wondering. What difference did it make to him, after all?

It was well after midnight when they climbed back into the van. Crunch put his arm around Didi. Her head fell to his shoulder, and in moments she was asleep.

Kent walked back to the dorm with them and said good-night once they were all inside. Queen Bea made an elaborate show of locking the door behind him. She hadn't troubled to hide her annoyance at their late return, but there wasn't anything she could say. Kent was in charge, and she'd known all along that on this one night, they'd be back very late.

Bea would have liked to make them go to bed, but she couldn't do that either. She stalked off to her apartment without so much as a "good-night."

Eve made for the pay telephone. "Who's she calling at this hour?" Didi asked Beth.

"Her parents," Beth replied. "She called them from the city, but there was no answer."

"Gee, I hope nothing's wrong," Didi said.

"Nothing's wrong," Beth explained. "She just talks to them every day. If she forgets to call them, they call her."

"Every day?" Didi could not conceal her amazement. Most of them had called their parents to say they'd arrived safely, or perhaps to ask for more money, but that was about all. Crunch hadn't even done that. His parents had left for Italy at about the same time he'd left for Hudson Manor.

"Her father spoke at our school once," Danny said. "He's famous."

"I know," Crunch said. "I saw him interviewed on TV. He's a historian or something."

"Yes," Danny said, as if somehow that explained Eve's attachment.

But it didn't, of course. Crunch had told himself to forget about Eve. Marla Romano, Antoinette Schaeffer, Ducky Alpaugh—all they'd gotten out of him was a poem apiece and a week's worth of dreaming, day and night dreaming. Eve didn't deserve a jot more. He wasn't interested in her romantically anymore, he told himself. Not at all. But she still intrigued him. Just as a case study. Unlike Rhonda's birth mother, Eve's father seemed to be a real, honest-to-goodness celebrity.

However, the phone was on the other side of the room. Crunch couldn't hear Eve's conversation without coming closer, and he wasn't about to do anything as obvious as that. When she hung up the phone, she called out, "Goodnight." Danny went off to his room a few moments later.

"I'll be back in a couple of minutes," Crunch said to Didi. "I just have to check something out."

Didi was stretched out on the floor beside him. "I'm not going anywhere," she said, shutting her eyes.

He knocked on the door to Danny's room. "Come on in," Danny called. Inside, Crunch found him seated at his desk, his typewriter open and paper in the platen.

"Don't you ever stop writing?" Crunch asked.

"Sure," Danny replied, snapping the notebook shut. "When I'm fooling around."

"Can you fool around with a girl," Crunch wondered, "if you met her father first?"

93

"You mean Eve? I don't see why not—but I haven't, if that's what you're asking. Not yet, anyway. Do I have your permission?"

"You don't need it," Crunch admitted.

"You're damn right."

Crunch sat down on the bed. "What's her father like? I know he won a Pulitzer prize."

"For a book called *The Death Machine*," Danny said. "It's about Treblinka."

"Treblinka? Oh, yeah, the concentration camp."

"The Nazis murdered hundreds of thousands of Jews there, and other people too, during World War Two. Dr. Streitman came out of Treblinka alive. Not too many people did." Danny reached up to the shelf above his head for a loose-leaf notebook. "Maybe I still have some stuff about Dr. Streitman in my English notebook. I saved everything." He flipped through the pages until he found what he was looking for, a sheet photocopied from a biographical dictionary. He snapped it out of the notebook and handed it to Crunch.

Crunch read it carefully.

Micah Streitman had been born in Prague in 1925, one of Elihu and Batya Kralovik Streitman's seven children. At sixteen, he along with his entire family had been interned by the Nazis, first at Theresienstadt and later at Treblinka. He was the only member of his family to survive the war. Liberated in 1945, he made his way to America, where he earned a B.A. at Columbia University in 1949 and a Ph.D. in 1953. He taught history at Johns Hopkins, UCLA, and the University of Michigan, returning to Columbia in 1973 as the Henry W. Dodgeson Professor of Modern European Intellectual History. He

94

was the author of several volumes seeking to discover in the history of German culture some kind of explanation for the triumph of Nazism, as well as many articles in both scholarly and popular magazines, and a critically acclaimed personal memoir entitled *Isaac My Father*. He'd been awarded a Pulitzer prize for *The Death Machine*, a definitive history of Treblinka. In 1969 he married Elena Baum, a physicist. They were the parents of one daughter, Eve, born in 1972.

Crunch looked up from the paper. "I guess he went through a lot, huh?"

Danny grimaced.

"What's that face supposed to mean?" Crunch asked.

"He experienced the worst evil the human race has ever known," Danny retorted, "and all you can say is 'I guess he went through a lot.'"

"What am I supposed to say?" Crunch snapped.

Danny threw his hands in the air. "I don't know. I guess no one does. Streitman tries because he was there. He managed to survive, and ever since he's been trying to figure out why. I suppose that's why he named his daughter Eve. In Hebrew her name would be Hava. That means 'life.'"

"The first woman."

Danny nodded.

"Have you read his books?" Crunch wondered.

"Yeah, though I skipped a lot."

"Boring?"

"No. Unbearable."

Unbearable in what way, Crunch thought, but he didn't ask. The thing about the evil in a horror novel was that you didn't have to believe in it. This was different.

"Do you want something else?" Danny asked.

"Not really. Thanks. Good night." Grunch left, glad to have learned more about Eve—though actually he'd learned nothing about her, only about her father. But knowing something about her father at least made him feel he could place her in a context.

What would he do with the information? He had no idea.

Tucking what he'd learned in the back of his mind, Crunch returned to the lounge, where Didi was waiting for him.

# Second Sunday

Crunch put a plastic bag over his cast and went swimming with Stu and James after lunch. Of course he couldn't actually swim, but it was nice on a breathlessly hot, silent summer afternoon to simply immerse himself in the water, to feel its cool greenness closing over his head. With feet tucked underneath him, he sank down to the concrete bottom like a catfish.

When he floated up to the surface, he realized that the three of them no longer had the pool to themselves. Sierra, wearing the briefest possible bikini, bounced lightly on the end of the board and then executed a flawless dive into the water. Three or four long, swift strokes brought her to his side. Holding on to the edge with one hand, she smoothed her short, dark hair with the other. James sat near them, his feet dangling in the water. Methodically, Stu swam back and forth from one end of the pool to the other, intent on accomplishing forty laps.

"I looked for you Friday night," Sierra said. "I couldn't find you."

"We assumed you were busy," James replied.

"I didn't stay long in Kent's room," she returned. "Did you think that I would?"

"Long enough to get whatever it is you wanted out of that wolf in a book reviewer's clothing," James retorted.

"He asked me to come. I couldn't have said no, could I? Not to a guest. It wouldn't have been polite."

James reached into the pool and splashed water in her face. "And God knows, Sierra, you're nothing if not polite."

"It was boring up there," Sierra said. "But then I couldn't find a way into the basement. When I came down from Kent's room, I wandered all over the first floor of Marygrove, looking for stairs. The ones from the kitchen were locked."

"You couldn't have gotten to where we were from the kitchen anyway," Crunch said. "The basement's in two parts. You could never find your way to where we were by yourself."

"I heard there's some kind of tomb down there. Did you guys have fun?"

Crunch shrugged.

"I'd like to see it. Will you take me down there tonight, Crunch?" Sierra asked. She lifted her eyebrows and smiled. It was a question and a promise.

"Of course he will," James replied quickly. Crunch turned to him, frowning. But James went right on talking. "You meet us on the veranda of Marygrove at eleven o'clock tonight. We'll take you down."

98

"You don't have to come," Sierra said. "I mean, you know, maybe you're busy."

James grinned. "Don't worry. Meg'll come too. There's plenty of room."

Crunch lifted his bad arm out of the water. "I've got to get out of here. I don't want this thing to get wet." He managed to hoist himself up the ladder with one hand.

"See you later," Sierra called. "See you at eleven o'clock."

Later, hearing noises across the hall, Crunch came out of his room and pushed open James's door. "What's the big idea?" he asked. "You can hang out with Sierra in the mausoleum tonight if you want to, but I'm not coming. I'd as soon fool around with her as I would with the witch in *Snow White*."

"Who's talking about fooling around?" James said.

"She is," Crunch said. "She's sick."

"One man's kink is another man's kicks," James returned easily.

"So okay," Crunch said. "Leave Meg home and meet her in the crypt yourself."

"I have a better idea," James said. "A much better idea."

That night they went to a movie in Milton. Didi grinned at Crunch and patted the place next to her as he climbed into the van.

"I'll sit in the back," Crunch said, putting on his pleasantest smile. "Let one of the girls have the comfortable seat." He didn't want Didi acting as if they were going together, like Stu and Linda. Their relationship wasn't anything more than friendship, with a little fooling around thrown in when the opportunity presented itself.

That's how it was for him, and that's how he wanted it to be for her.

A moment later Sierra stepped in, carrying a large paper bag. "Hey, Rhonda," she called, "I brought you a present."

"You mean all is forgiven?" Rhonda said, reaching for the bag. "Good!"

"You love hats so much," Sierra went on, "I made this one especially for you."

Eagerly Rhonda pulled it out of the bag. Her smile disappeared as she stared at the tall, pointed cap she held in her hand. It was made out of red cardboard, and written on it in large black letters was the word DUNCE.

"Put it on," Sierra said. "You'll look stunning."

"Honestly, Sierra," James said, "can't you take what was just a joke?" He grabbed the dunce cap from Rhonda's hand, threw it on the floor of the van, and stomped on it.

Just then Kent arrived, followed by Enid. Nothing more was said about the incident, but no one spoke to Sierra all the way to Milton. Rhonda shut her eyes and pretended to be asleep.

In the theater Crunch did sit next to Didi. He was on the aisle, where he had room for his long legs. On the other side of Didi sat Rhonda, and next to her was Beth. The others found places in the row in front of them. They giggled through the latest episode of *Friday the 13th,* and when it was over, Beth said, "We should have gone to see that French film, like Kent wanted us to. This stuff just doesn't scare me anymore. I didn't have to shut my eyes once."

"I hate being scared," Eve said. "I just hate it. I never go to horror movies at home."

"So what did you come tonight for?" Beth asked.

"I wasn't going to stay in the dorm all by myself, was I?" Eve replied. "That would have been worse."

"I wasn't scared either," Sierra said. "But then I'm never scared."

Didi whispered to Crunch. "If there's anything I hate more than horror films, it's Sierra McCaughey."

"We'll see how brave she is tonight," Crunch whispered back.

"What do you mean?"

"I'll tell you in a minute."

He waited until the row in front was vacant, and then he told Beth and Rhonda too. "I'm coming," Beth said. "This I have to see."

"Me too," said Didi.

"You couldn't keep me away," Rhonda agreed.

"Just make sure you get out in time," Crunch warned.

They met on the veranda of Marygrove shortly before eleven. Sierra arrived a few minutes later. "This was just supposed to be me and Crunch and James and Meg," she complained.

"Tough," Didi retorted.

"The crypt belongs to all of us," Beth said.

Crunch's tone was conciliatory. "You missed Friday night. We're going to do it again, for you."

They moved around to the side of the building. Crunch and James held the rhododendron bushes back so the girls could pass between them. James unlocked the cellar door and put the padlock and key in his pocket. Crunch entered first, lighting the way with his flashlight. Unhesitat-

101

ingly the others followed. Except for Sierra they knew where they were going.

They made their way down the corridor. Sierra said something, but her comments were ignored, and soon she stopped making them. The only sound was footsteps scraping against the ground. When they reached the end of the hall, James pushed open the door to the mausoleum. One by one they entered the room, ranging themselves along the wall as Crunch moved his light slowly from one object to another, illuminating the pictures first, and then the brass candelabra, and finally the enormous sarcophagus. Still no one spoke.

Sierra uttered a high-pitched giggle. "It's something," she said. "It's really something."

"Are you afraid, Sierra?" James asked. His voice, deep and hollow, seemed to rise from the pit of his belly.

"Of course not," she said. "Why should I be afraid of an empty tomb?"

"Are you sure it's empty?" James asked.

"And what if it isn't?" Sierra returned. "Why should I be afraid of some old bones?"

"I don't know," James said. "Why don't you open the box and find out what's in it?"

Sierra giggled again. "I'm sure it's sealed."

"You won't know unless you try."

Sierra didn't move. Crunch's flashlight remained fixed on the sarcophagus. "You *are* afraid," James said.

"I am not," Sierra insisted.

"Then open the coffin. Go ahead."

"You do it."

"But *I'm* afraid," James said. "I don't deny it."

Hesitantly Sierra moved away from the wall. Then she

threw back her shoulders, lifted her chin, and marched briskly toward the cement box. Scurrying like mice, the girls slipped out of the room. James left too and stood behind the door, his hand flat against the upper panel. Crunch remained in the doorway, his light still fixed on the center of the room.

Sierra put her hand on the lid of the sarcophagus. "Good night, Sierra," Crunch said softly. He switched off his light and retreated quickly through the doorway. James slammed the door shut and snapped the padlock in place.

"Hey," Sierra shouted, "what's the big idea?"

"Good night, Sierra." This time Crunch called the words out in a voice loud enough for her to hear through the door.

"Good night, Sierra," James echoed.

"Let me out of here, you jerks," Sierra cried. "Let me out right now."

Crunch had switched his light on again as soon as James had closed the door. The two of them started down the hall. Didi and Meg walked with them.

"Where are you going?" Beth called after them.

Crunch paused and turned. "Back to the dorm."

"And then you're going to come all the way back here to let her out?" Beth asked. "That's silly. Just wait here ten minutes."

"Ten minutes?" Meg snorted. "Ten minutes won't do any good. She's got to stay there an hour or two. Maybe all night."

"I think that's too long," Beth said. "Really, Meg, I think it's too long."

"An hour or so is not too long," James said. "It's just right."

"You have to let her out sometime. If you wait too long,

she'll tell Randy Rory and Queen Bea," Rhonda warned. "We'll get into a lot of trouble." Her eyes widened with a new, apparently disturbing thought. "She may tell Rory and Bea anyway. Or even Kent and Enid."

"I'll take the blame," James said. "It doesn't make any difference to me if I get thrown out."

"But I don't want to get thrown out," Beth said.

"I told you, I'll take the blame," James repeated.

"Ten minutes is a joke. Two hours is not." Beth marched forward and put out her hand. "Give me the key."

James shook his head.

"Oh, Beth, don't be a wimp," Meg said. "Come on, let's get out of here."

Suddenly Sierra's shouting and banging ceased. In response to her unexpected silence, they too stopped speaking. "You're still there," Sierra said. "I know you're still there. Well, you have to let me out sometime."

"We do?" James called back. "Wait and see."

"I don't care when it is," Sierra retorted. "I'm going to sleep. Good night."

"We can leave her," Didi whispered. "She's all right."

"Well, if she's all right, what's the point of leaving her?" Rhonda said. "She's supposed to be frightened. If she's not frightened, we might as well let her out."

"Oh, she'll get frightened," James said quietly. "Once we're gone. That's why we've got to go."

"Not me," Rhonda said. "I'm not leaving."

"Hey, Rhonda," Crunch said lightly, "we did this for you."

"No, you didn't," Rhonda said. "You thought it up before tonight. So don't blame me."

"Crunch, you told too many people," Meg complained. "It was a mistake."

104

"Leave, all of you," Sierra called. "I don't give a damn."

"You don't mean that," Rhonda shouted.

"Of course I mean it," Sierra grumbled. "You're bastards. Every one of you. That includes you, Rhonda Tulipano."

"My God, she really is impossible," Crunch exclaimed.

"Look, Rhonda, you wait here," Beth said. "I'll get my flashlight and come right back."

"Boy, Beth, you're a total wimp," Meg said. "I never realized what an infant you are."

"I'm not a wimp," Beth retorted. "If I were, I'd be banging on Rory and Bea's door. But I'm not going to do that. So consider yourselves fortunate." She ran past them. They whirled and hurried after her.

A brilliant moon lit the path that led from Marygrove to the dorm. Strolling toward them in the silver light were Eve and Danny, their heads bent close in conversation. But not touching, Crunch had time to notice. No hands held; no arms entwined. Just talking, that's all.

Eve saw Beth first. "What's the matter?" she exclaimed. "You look furious."

"I am furious. But I have no time to explain. I need a flashlight."

Danny reached into his pocket. "Here, take mine."

"Thanks," she returned briefly. She spun around and headed back toward Marygrove. Eve hurried to catch up with her. "What's the matter? Tell me."

"These crazy guys have locked Sierra in the crypt. Without a light."

"Hey!" Crunch exclaimed. "That's not fair. You were right there with us."

"Yes, the more fool I. But I thought you were going to lock her in there for two seconds and let her out again."

"Two seconds, two hours . . ." Crunch began. Beth did not stay to listen to what he was saying.

And anyway, he never finished. Something had happened to Eve. Crunch had never seen her like this. Usually so cool and remote, her face now flushed with furious passion, her eyes blazed with untrammeled fire. Without warning, she raised clenched fists and struck Crunch's chest with a succession of blows that were actually painful. "Let her out," she cried. "Right now, let her out."

He grabbed her wrists. "Calm down, Eve. What's the matter with you?"

"I said let her out." Eve screamed.

Still holding Eve, Crunch glanced at James. "Maybe we'd better."

"Just because Eve says so?" James retorted.

Eve took advantage of Crunch's distraction to free herself from his grasp. She confronted James like an avenging goddess. "Let her out," she said. She lifted her long fingernails to his face. "You torturer. You fascist torturer."

Again Crunch put his hands on her arms. "Don't, Eve."

Eve was sobbing now, great gulping sobs. James stepped back, reached in his pocket, pulled out the key, and handed it to Crunch. "You're crazy, Eve," he said. "You're really crazy."

"Torturers," Eve repeated. "A bunch of torturers."

James turned away, and with Didi and Meg in tow, he strolled toward the dormitory. Crunch headed for Marygrove, Eve, wiping her nose and eyes with her fingers, at his side. Now he was furious too and made no effort to hide it. "What do you mean, 'fascist torturer'?" he exclaimed.

"Just because your father is the big expert on concentration camps is no reason to call me names." So many branches of the rhododendrons had been broken by frequent passages through that this time Crunch didn't even have to push them aside.

"Leave my father out of this," she insisted as she followed him down the cement stairs.

"Your father's famous. Everyone knows about him." Not quite everyone, Crunch realized. A Pulitzer Prize–winning historian was not the same thing as an Oscar–winning movie actor. But famous enough so that an interested person could catch his face in the newspaper or on a TV news show and maybe remember it.

At the far end of the corridor Crunch could see the beam of the flashlight Beth was carrying. "Have you brought the key?" Beth called, her voice echoing through the vaulted hallway as if she were standing at the bottom of a pit.

Eve began to run. "Is Sierra all right?" she cried. She placed her mouth as close to the crack between the door and the door jamb as she could get it. "Sierra!" she shouted. "How are you?"

"I'm fine," Sierra returned, her voice perhaps even more self-satisfied than usual. "Just fine."

Crunch pushed the key into the padlock. Rhonda grabbed the knob and pulled the door open. Sierra stepped out into the light. "You bastards," she said.

"Yeah, we know," Crunch said. "You already told us."

"Goddamn bastards."

"There's gratitude," Crunch returned. "We're the ones who let you out, and what's our reward? You curse us."

"You're also the ones who put me in," Sierra said. "I

107

guess I know where I stand now, if I didn't before. You can all drop dead so far as I'm concerned." She turned to Beth. "Give me a light."

Beth handed her the flashlight. "It's Danny's," she said.

Turning her back on them, Sierra stalked down the hall. "She's all right," Rhonda said. "Nothing's changed."

Beth's gaze was fixed on Eve. "But you're not all right," she said. She put her arm around Eve, whose body was shaking as if she were suffering from a hundred and four degrees of fever.

"Maybe Sierra isn't all right either," Eve said. "You don't know. You can't know."

"I don't understand," Crunch said. "What's the matter with you, Eve? You're acting like you were the one who got locked in the tomb. Sierra's no friend of yours."

"Whether or not she's a friend of mine," Eve retorted, "has nothing to do with it. You did a terrible thing. A sickening thing."

Crunch shook his head. "Maybe it wasn't the greatest idea in the world, but you're overreacting. Really, you are." He turned to the others. "Isn't she?"

But Beth and Rhonda did not reply. He couldn't tell where they stood.

"All right," Eve said, "just step in here. It's the right place for what I need to tell you." She entered the crypt; the others followed. She shut the door and then sat down on the threadbare carpet, motioning to the others to do the same. "Shut out your light, Crunch," she ordered.

He obeyed. He didn't know why. Her voice carried such authority that he felt he must do as she said. He wondered what was going to happen next.

For a while, nothing. The blackness and the silence

seemed to weigh on him like lead. He needed to act as if he didn't feel it; he needed to push it away. "Now I know how old Erastus feels," he said. "I mean, if he's in there."

Rhonda responded with a nervous giggle. "No, you don't," Beth said. "He's dead. He doesn't feel anything."

"Being dead isn't scary," Eve said. "It's the dying that's scary."

Crunch remembered Friday night. The lightness left his voice. "Is that what you're afraid of, Eve? Dying?"

"I have this dream. I dream it over and over again," Eve said. "I see a subway. I'm supposed to meet someone who's on it, someone I care about a lot. But I never make it. The train is always pulling away from the platform just as I get there. I've tried to figure out that dream. I think the person I'm supposed to meet must be dead. But I don't know who that person is. That dream scares me. I'm afraid of not knowing who the dead person is, and I'm afraid of knowing too."

She paused for a moment, and when she began to speak again, her voice was so low that Crunch had to strain to hear it. But he caught every word. "Have you ever been awakened in the middle of the night by someone crying? I'm afraid of the next time I'm startled out of my sleep by the sound of my father's sobs, and my mother's voice trying to comfort him, as if she were his mother. I'm afraid of the unspeakable pain locked in their memories. I'm afraid their memories will become my memories. I'm afraid of their incurable, unending sadness, which I fear will become my sadness. That's what I'm afraid of."

"What are their memories?" Beth asked. Her voice was a whisper in the pitchlike darkness.

"My father was at Treblinka." Eve's voice was tight and

flat. "The Nazis brought him there. He was seventeen. The rest of his family had already died at Theresienstadt. Except his baby sister. When she was three, my father watched the soldiers kill her the day the Jews of his district were rounded up. Something distracted my grandmother, and she let go of the baby's hand. That little girl was very smart. She knew something terrible was happening. She ran, so they shot her. In front of her mother."

Crunch heard Beth and Rhonda gasp. His own stomach lurched, as if he were going to throw up.

"But that was nothing," Eve continued. "Nothing. When the railroad car into which they'd locked my father and I don't know how many other people arrived at Treblinka, half of them were dead. My father had spent three days without food and water, with no place to relieve himself, in the company of a graveyard of rotting corpses."

"Okay," Crunch said. "We get the picture. We understand."

Eve seemed not to have heard him. "He survived the camps because he was young, but not too young, and healthy. Even though he had almost nothing to eat, and no shoes to wear, even in the middle of winter, he could work. So they let him live. He made friends with some people at the beginning, but not later on. What was the point? Sooner or later they were sent to the showers. That's what they were called, showers. People pretended not to know what happened there, only they really did know. Because of the smoke from the chimneys. The endless smoke. And the stench of course. The smell of burning flesh. He got used to that. That was the worst part. He got used to it."

Crunch put his hand over his mouth. He felt as if he were going to throw up.

"And you know what bothers him the most? You know what memory is the hardest for him to live with?" Eve actually laughed, a grim and bitter laugh. "Toward the end of the war, a second cousin of his actually showed up at the same camp. Everyone had a ration card. That's how they got their rotten potato each day, and their cup of gruel. By this time my father was very sick. It was winter. He probably had pneumonia. Of course there was no medical treatment. He had to keep on working too, because if he didn't, he knew where he'd end up. Well, anyway, someone came to tell him his cousin had died. So he rushed over there and threw himself on top of his cousin's body, weeping and moaning. They thought he was sobbing with grief. But he didn't really care about his cousin. See, that's why the Nazis were able to do what they did. They dehumanized you, and then they killed you. That way, they didn't have to feel guilty.

"My father was pretending. All the while he was lying on the corpse, he was feeling in the pockets for his cousin's ration card. And when he found it, he hid it in his own clothes and went away. He was able to get double portions from then on—enough to live on. *Two* rotten potatoes, so he survived. That bothers him the most because he says he had become like them, like the Nazis. That was the worst thing the Nazis did to the inmates of the camps—they robbed them of their humanity."

Crunch didn't want to hear any more. He didn't want to hear another word. He groped for his flashlight. His fingers curled around it as tightly as if it were a life preserver, and he switched it on.

Eve was sobbing. Beth's arm was around her. Rhonda was staring at her with stricken eyes. "So now you know,"

111

Eve said. "Now you can be afraid of what I'm afraid of. Only you won't be, will you? Because it's not your parents. It's just one of ten million stories that don't seem real."

Crunch climbed to his feet. He wanted to get out of the crypt more than he'd ever wanted anything else in his life. He wanted to get out of the cellar before he stopped breathing. The others followed him. They had no choice. He held the light.

He remembered to shut and padlock the cellar door. But then he ran away from them as if the devil himself were at his heels. In the dormitory lounge he found Didi, drinking soda with Linda, Stu, and Martina. The four of them were laughing about something. Sierra maybe.

"Hey, Didi," Crunch said, "you want to go for a walk?" With an effort he forced his voice into its normal register.

"Sure," Didi said. "Why not?" She turned to the others. "You guys coming?"

Crunch didn't wait for their answer. He pulled on Didi's hand, dragging her out the door. He put his arm around her shoulder and kissed her on the neck. She giggled and turned her head so that her lips grazed his cheek.

He held her face between his hands and kissed her. Didi's eyes were smooth, shallow pools. No burden of memory lay like a shadow beneath their surface. He kissed her again and again. If he kissed her enough, he could erase Eve's eyes and Eve's words from his mind. He didn't want to think about them, ever again. He didn't want to believe that they were true.

# Second Monday

Eve was afraid to go to sleep that night. She was sure the dream would come again. Perhaps this time the hidden identity of the train's ghost passenger might be revealed. She felt quite certain she'd rather not know, and she stayed up reading for as long as she could, falling asleep unawares, with the lamp still lit. So far as she could remember when she awoke, she hadn't dreamt at all. So the dreams that had visited her when she was too deeply asleep to be aware of them hadn't been nightmares about the subway. She was sure such dreams always awakened her, no matter how far sunk into unconsciousness she was when she dreamt them. Under Marygrove Sunday night she'd exposed much more of herself than ever before—not all, of course, but so much more. And yet the dream had stayed away. She was surprised, and grateful.

She'd overslept and missed breakfast. She dressed

quickly, grabbed her notebook, and ran past shouting day campers to the classroom building. The others seemed not to notice her as she slipped quietly into her accustomed seat in the English resource room. They were too busy listening to Enid.

Enid knew. The assignment she was making provided convincing evidence. Again Eve was surprised. She had thought Sierra, though furious, would not tell, especially since she had insisted she was unafraid. It must be, then, that Sierra wasn't most angry at being locked in the creepiest room this side of Dracula's castle. She was most angry at realizing with absolute finality that she was the group's outcast. After all, Rhonda's practical joke had been forgiven; Sierra's retaliation had not been.

And in telling Enid, Sierra had solidified her unenviable position. She was really bright, certainly talented, and even good-looking. It was hard for Eve to believe that such a person simply didn't have the faintest idea of how to behave among her own peers. Or maybe, on the profoundest level, she just didn't care what they thought of her. That was even harder to believe. A kid might choose to go her own way, might deliberately adhere to values her contemporaries didn't share, but to do so without pain—from her own experience, Eve simply couldn't accept that. Some part of Sierra must be hurting. But she had rejected Beth, Rhonda, and Eve herself so vehemently the night before that Eve felt she had no choice but to back off. With all her heart she wished the whole terrible evening had never happened.

Enid was making such a pretense impossible. Usually she handed out photocopies of the day's writing exercise. Today she delivered her instructions orally, her face wiped clean of what Eve had thought to be her sewn-on smile. Enid told them to write their own accounts of the previous night's events. She didn't say what those events were, but she instructed them to include the reasons for their own behavior, as well as the behavior of others. "And when you're talking about why other people acted as they did," she said sharply, "make sure you tell us what evidence you have to support your understanding of their motivations."

Eve clutched her pen tightly in her fingers. "I don't want to do this," she said. "I'm not going to do it."

"Why, Eve?" Enid said. She seemed genuinely startled. "From what I understand, you're one of the few people whose behavior last night was above reproach."

"If I don't mind writing about it," Sierra said, "I don't see why you should."

"I don't want to write about what I did last night, or what I thought." Eve felt her face turn hot, but she did not lower her glance.

"You never want to write about anything that really matters, do you, Eve?" The smile had returned to Enid's lips, and her voice was almost gentle.

"I don't much want to write about it either," Crunch said.

"I don't care whether you want to or not," Enid returned. "It's what you're going to do—all of you."

"What is this?" James queried. "Some kind of punishment?"

"You can call it that if you want to," Enid replied drily.

"Some of us weren't even there," Linda protested.

"You were somewhere. You heard about it beforehand, or you were in the dorm when those involved returned from Marygrove. What did you do when you found out? You can all write about that."

They smiled, Eve remembered. Some of them even laughed. Sierra had gone to her room as soon as she came in, but after curfew, when the couples had returned to the dorm from their evening make-out sessions, the rest of them sat around in the lounge. "So what happened?" Danny had wanted to know. "What did you need my flashlight for?"

"We locked Sierra in the crypt," Beth admitted. "Rhonda and I wanted to let her out right away. Crunch and James didn't."

"Serves her right." Meg remained unrepentant. "The crypt is where she belongs."

"It's an awful place," Rhonda said.

"I don't think it's so bad," Didi said. "It's like, well, it's like different."

"It didn't bother Sierra to be there," James said. "It bothered Eve that we put her there. She decided we're all Nazis."

"That's not what I said," Eve retorted.

"It's what you meant."

"Did you?" Didi turned to Eve. "You know that's ridiculous."

Beth rose to Eve's defense. "You take one person and make her the scapegoat. You punish her not because she's done anything bad to you, but just because, for some reason or other, you don't like her."

"Sierra did something bad to Rhonda," Didi said.

"And I did something bad to Sierra," Rhonda replied quietly. "So we were even."

"You're blaming the victim for what happened," Beth

116

said. "It was her own fault, you're saying. She didn't act right. That's just what Nazis did."

"Nazis were cruel," Martina said. "They killed people."

"Locking Sierra in the room was cruel," Beth said. "I'm sorry I had anything to do with it."

"But you're missing the point," Crunch cried. "The Nazis killed their victims. Sierra wasn't even hurt."

Once again Eve found herself unable to maintain superficial control. She rose to her feet and marched over to him, standing in front of him and staring down into his wide, untroubled, infuriating eyes. "If you'd left her there, who knows what might have happened? You were stopped, thank goodness. And that's the real difference between you and a guard in a concentration camp. Maybe the only difference. You were stopped."

"Cut it out, Eve," Crunch returned, his voice low. "You're overreacting again."

Her brain issued no command of which she was conscious, but as if it were something separate from the rest of her, behaving according to its own will, her hand swung back and then forward, striking Crunch sharply on the cheek.

And then the hand returned and covered Eve's open mouth. Earlier she'd pounded his chest. Now she'd slapped his cheek. She could never have imagined doing such things, and yet she had done them. "I'm sorry," she whispered. She turned and ran from the room.

Beth followed her. "Look, Eve," she said, "it was all right. He deserved it."

"The way Sierra deserved to be imprisoned? If anyone deserved it, it was James. But it wasn't James that I hit." Eve sunk down onto her bed and put her head into her hands. "My God, Beth, what's happening to me here? I'm losing control."

"Does that always have to be a bad thing?" Beth wondered.

Eve had stared at her. "Yes," she had said. "Always. Always and forever."

And now, in class on a clear, shadowless Monday morning, Eve found herself on guard. Maybe when you're asleep you can't watch yourself, she thought, and so you dream. But when you're awake you can, every second. "Do you have to turn everything into a writing exercise?" she protested to Enid. "Even what went on here last night?"

"If it's a punishment," James said, "I have a better idea. Send me home. I was the ringleader."

Kent spoke up. "We thought of that, but we dismissed it."

"Why?"

"Maybe because you want to go home."

James ran his fingers through his mass of thick blond curls. "Lord, this is a crazy place." He turned to Crunch. "You still want out of here?"

Crunch took a deep breath. "I wouldn't mind."

Kent leaned over and whispered something to Enid. Enid nodded. Kent stood up. He was well over six feet tall, and though thin, his height, combined with his military bearing, provided him with an authoritative presence when he needed it. "I sense incipient rebellion here," he announced in firm, even tones. "Until now Enid and I have agreed that this conference shouldn't be the same as school. We have considered this group as if it were a

118

community of artists in which all of us, including Enid and myself, are peers—more experienced perhaps than the rest of you, but not your superiors in any absolute sense. Well, last night's episode suggests that our trust was misplaced. You've forfeited the right to be treated as adults. For the time being, at least, you can regard Enid and me as your teachers, with all the authority that term usually conveys."

"The other was a pretense all along," Meg interjected. "It always is when teachers act like kids are their buddies. Do one thing they don't like, and the game is up."

"It wasn't a pretense," Enid said. "It was a mistake. We assumed you were adults. Last night proved us wrong."

Eve felt a hot wave of anger roll over her. How dare Enid imply that all cruelty resided in kids? The Nazis who'd robbed her father and mother of their youth and the rest of her relatives of their very lives hadn't been children. Even if children could think up things as ghastly as what the Nazis had done, they were powerless to execute them. Powerlessness. Kids always, like Europe's Jews for centuries and centuries, were powerless. Why were those with power so frightened by the slightest sign of rebellion among the powerless, among those who in actuality could do nothing? "All right," she said to Enid, "I'll do the assignment." Perhaps she'd be able to say something all the others needed to hear. It was her obligation.

"Crunch?" Enid asked.

He shrugged, and she seemed to take that as acquiescence. She glanced at her watch as she rose to her feet. "I'll see you back here in an hour. I'm giving you more time than usual. You have a bigger job." She sat down at a table on which she'd set up her portable electronic typewriter. She and Kent usually did the assignments too, or at least seemed to. Eve had no idea of what they actually wrote.

In the little classroom where she usually worked, Eve sat alone and pondered an empty sheet of paper. Feeling extremely warm, she rose and opened the windows. It was hot out; that didn't help much. She pulled down the shades. Though the air was almost motionless, now and then a shade flapped. The clock on the wall moved inexorably forward.

In front of her eyes she saw the crypt. She saw the sarcophagus. And she remembered her dream, the one she'd expected to have the night before, the one which, miraculously, had never come. She picked up her pen and began to write.

Later, back in the resource room, each of them read their papers, one by one. When it was Eve's turn, it seemed to her that the words stuck in her throat. But she pushed them out, like a mother bird throwing fledglings from the nest.

Sometimes I dream. Sometimes at night, I dream. The dream is often the same, or nearly so. I dream that I must meet a subway train. I have to pick up someone who's on it, someone about whom I care a great deal, though I can never quite remember the name. I run down the steps into the station. But I'm too late. The train I'm supposed to meet is gone.

I run to the next station, but the same thing happens. I arrive underground just in time to see the lights of the train receding down the track. My desperation grows. I run from station to station to station. I become increasingly convinced that something terrible has happened. I will never see the person on the train again.

To describe what I'm doing cannot begin to convey what I'm feeling. What I'm feeling has no apparent relationship to my actions or to the setting. I'm shaking, my hands are clammy, my skin prickles with goose bumps. It is as if the train I'm chasing is not the Broadway line I've ridden almost every day since I was six. It's as if it were the closed railroad car my father rode to Treblinka. My terror is so great that it's only with great effort that I force myself to keep running, running, running.

I never find out why I can't meet the person who's on the train. Or at least, I never could, before last night. Last night I figured it out. Last night I understood. The person on the train, whoever he or she is—that person is dead.

She put the notebook down in her lap and glanced at Enid. Slowly, unsmilingly, Enid nodded. The room was absolutely silent. Not a paper rustled. Not a pencil tapped. A minute or two passed before Enid spoke, a moment that seemed as long as a year. "Thank you, Eve," Enid said. "Does anyone have anything to say about what Eve has written?"

No one answered. Beth reached out, took Eve's hand, and squeezed it. Eve was surprised but glad; the touch seemed to steady her. It helped the trembling cease.

121

Kent began to talk about the rhythm of Eve's piece. Enid praised its use of action to convey emotion. Linda noted its effective handling of repetition. "How can you talk about it as if it's just another paragraph?" Martina exclaimed. "A person pours out her soul and you act as if it's just another exercise. How can you be so cold and analytical?"

"So far, no one's done anything but praise it," Stu said. "I don't call that cold."

"It does have shape," Danny said. "It uses the devices of art. I think it's fair to treat it, on one level, simply as a piece of writing."

Martina threw up her hands. "I don't think I'll ever make a writer. I can't stand off from myself and look at myself as if I were a tree or something. It seems to me that's what you guys expect a writer to do. Feel all these emotions, and then treat them like they were eggs, just meant to be cracked and baked into a cake."

"Anyway," Didi said, "I don't see what it has to do with last night."

Crunch banged his fist on the seat of his chair. "To Eve, it has everything to do with last night!" he exclaimed. "She takes everything so personally."

"Crunch, calm yourself," Enid said. "Just tell us what you mean."

"I'll read you what I wrote instead."

"Fine," Enid returned. "Another first. Go ahead."

Crunch picked up his notebook. "All right," he said. "Here goes."

I helped lock Sierra in the mausoleum in the basement of Marygrove. It's a pretty scary place, but it

122

isn't real. I don't believe Erastus Grove is actually buried there. There's a stone with his name on it in the cemetery next to Holy Innocents Episcopal Church, and I'm sure that's where his body is too.

Locking Sierra in the room wasn't nice, but it did no harm. Eve seems to think we acted like Nazis. Nazis were terrible human beings. As a matter of fact, I'm not sure they were really human beings at all. They wanted to rule the world and destroy everyone who stood in their way. They made Alexander the Great, Genghis Khan, and Napoleon look like Sunday school teachers. We had to fight a whole world war, in which millions died, just to get rid of them. I am not a Nazi; I am nothing like a Nazi.

Why does Eve hang on to these Nazis as if instead of being her father's enemies, they'd been his best friends? Why does anybody hang on to them? President Reagan got a lot of criticism for visiting a cemetery where German soldiers are buried. I think he did the right thing. The Nazis are gone. The Second World War has been over for a long time. We ought to forget about it and devote our energy to solving the problems that face us now.

Crunch lifted his head, and Eve saw the challenge in his eyes. "You don't understand," she said.

"I'm just telling you what I think," he returned. "You don't believe anyone can understand."

"Maybe Danny does, a little."

"You mean, because he's Jewish?"

Eve nodded. "I think any Jew who really knows he's

Jewish feels a little bit like a survivor." She turned to Danny.

He shrugged. "Maybe."

"But they can't know the whole of it," she said. "And who would want them to? I can't know it either. It didn't happen to me. It happened to my parents. It's just that the closer you get to it, the more you have to feel it, whether you want to or not."

"That's it," Crunch said. "You're saying you're more sensitive than me. You're saying you feel more than me. You're saying you're better than me."

Eve leaned back in her chair and shook her head. "I never said that." She realized she wasn't even angry any longer. How could you be angry at a fool? "I give up," she added without even raising her voice. "You're right about one thing. I don't think you understand *anything*. There's no point in talking to you."

"And there's no point in talking to you," he shot back. "We agree on that too." He ticked days off on his fingers. "Tuesday, Wednesday, Thursday, Friday. Four more days, that's all. We don't have to say another word to each other."

"My God," Stu sighed. "This jolly little group has sure fallen apart. Now some of us aren't even speaking."

Enid scratched her nose. "Let's play a game."

Rhonda groaned. "That's just what we need, a game."

Enid whispered something to Kent. He nodded, rose, and disappeared into his office. Enid arranged three chairs in a kind of circle in the middle of the group. "Okay, James," she announced. "Sit in this chair. You take this one, Beth. And Linda, you over here."

Beth and Linda immediately did as she asked. James

124

hesitated for a moment, then shrugged and obeyed. Kent returned, carrying a covered cardboard box immediately recognizable as the former residence of a pair of Reebok sneakers. He placed the box on the floor in front of James. "This box," Enid said, "pretend it's the sarcophagus down there in the Erastus Grove Memorial Chapel. The three of you are in the room with it." She mimed a door's slamming. "Bang! A wind blows the door shut. James runs, tries to open it, but it's locked from the outside. You're stuck in here until someone realizes you're missing and starts a search. Who knows when that'll be, or if they'll even think of searching the cellar of Marygrove?" Her smile looked like the Cheshire cat's. "What happens next?" She leaned back in her chair, as if she were watching a play in a theater.

James leaned back too and shut his eyes. Beth and Linda looked at each other, each waiting for the other to say something. Beth opened her mouth first. Eve had known that would happen. As nature abhors a vacuum, Beth abhorred silence. "We have to open the box," she said.

"We can't," Linda answered quietly. "The lid's solid granite. It weighs at least a ton."

James's eyelids fluttered. "What do we want to open it for anyway?" he asked, his drawl even more pronounced than usual.

"I think it has a false bottom," Beth said. "Maybe it leads to an underground passage that'll get us out of here, one of those tunnels they had before the Civil War to smuggle slaves to Canada." They were making up a story, the way they had the first night Crunch and James had brought them down to the mausoleum.

125

"Can't be. Marygrove couldn't have been built much before 1870. You can tell that from all the carved stone gingerbread." James was a good deal smarter than he cared to let on, with a lot of surprising information tucked away in his brain. "I wouldn't open that box if I were you. There's something terrible in that box."

Beth leaned toward him. "What is it, James? What's in the box?"

"Contrary to Crunch's opinion, Erastus Grove is not buried beneath the stone that bears his name in Holy Innocents churchyard. He's buried in that coffin." James stretched his hand toward the sneaker box. "Of course, his body is just bones now. But the knife blade is made of iron. It hasn't decayed."

"The knife blade!" Linda gasped. Eve couldn't tell if Linda was really shocked, or merely acting.

James nodded slowly. "Yes," he said. "The knife blade. Erastus Grove was murdered. I know who the murderer was, too."

"Who?" Linda asked.

"His supposedly adoring wife, Mary."

"And the motive? Do you also know that?" Beth queried drily.

"Oh, he did terrible things to her. Terrible things, in the privacy of their bedroom." James grinned like a crocodile. "Unspeakable things. Shall I spell them out?"

"That won't be necessary," Linda said.

Sierra rose and tapped James on the shoulder. Reluctantly he relinquished his seat. "Just when this was starting to be fun," he said.

Sierra took James's place. "Erastus Grove isn't in the coffin," she said. "I know who is." She rubbed her hands

126

together, as if she were washing them. "Not today—today it's empty. I'm talking about this time next year. If you open that box this time next year, you know what you'll find in it? The rotting flesh of James Birmingham."

Didi giggled. Sierra glared at her. "Crunch too," she added. "I put them there—lured them into the room, and then persuaded them to try out the coffin. You know, let's find out how it feels to be dead. Something like that. But I didn't kill them first. I just buried them alive."

So much, Eve thought, for Sierra's not caring. Crunch replaced Linda, enabling him to offer Sierra a kind of apology. "Maybe I did a lousy thing," he said. "But murder? Do you think I deserved that?"

"Maybe I didn't mean for you to die. That just happened," Sierra said. "Maybe I just wanted you to know how being locked up felt."

"You didn't act scared," Crunch said.

He was a fool, Eve thought. He really was. A fool, or a simpleton.

"I wouldn't give you the satisfaction," Sierra said. "And I wasn't scared," she added defiantly. "Not really."

Eve knew she was lying—a forgivable lie. Other than imagined murder, it was her only defense.

Stu took Sierra's place. Martina followed Beth; Rhonda followed Martina. Danny tapped Crunch out, Didi removed Martina, Meg followed Stu. They'd each taken a turn, each offering increasingly bizarre suggestions as to what the box contained.

Eve alone made no move to participate. "Well, Eve," Enid said at last. "What's your theory about the contents of that coffin?"

"I have no theory," she replied quietly. "These imagined horrors—they seem pointless to me. There are so many real ones."

"Wouldn't you like to know what's in the box—what's really in the box?" Crunch asked.

"I thought we weren't speaking," she returned sharply.

He shrugged and spread out his palms.

"It's like my dream," she said. "I want to know the name of the dead person on the train, and I don't want to know."

"Maybe," Crunch said, "maybe someday you'll have to know."

She stared at him. Suddenly he no longer seemed either a fool or a simpleton. "Yes," she whispered. "Maybe someday I will."

# Second Tuesday

Didi put her hand under Crunch's chin and lifted his face toward hers. "What's eating you, buddy?" she asked.

"Nothing," he returned soberly.

"That is the biggest lie I ever heard." She dropped her hand and turned away. "Here we are, all alone, under this huge oak tree, the moonlight flickering through the leaves, and what're you doing? Staring off into space like a mental case. I mean, if that's what you want to do, you can do it alone, you don't need me."

He put his arm around her and kissed her. Back in the dorm he'd thought he'd wanted to fool around, but no sooner did he get her where he supposedly wanted her than all desire seemed to have evaporated. Kissing her was nice; he couldn't deny that. But to press on with it—he just didn't have the energy. This wasn't like him. It wasn't like him at all. Was he all through at sixteen and a half?

Didi pulled away. "You're just kissing me because you think you ought to," she said. "You're not really interested."

"Of course I am," he replied vehemently. But of course he wasn't. He knew he wasn't. He still couldn't get Eve out of his mind, Eve and her stories. "Imagined horrors seem so pointless," she had said. "There are enough real ones." He almost hated Eve. She'd ruined Hudson Manor for him.

Didi stood up and fluffed out her hair. "We might as well go back."

"Why? Nothing doing there."

"Nothing doing here either," Didi returned coldly. "I'm going anyway. You can come or not, your choice."

Silently they walked back along the same moonlit path they'd followed out. Only this time, Crunch didn't bother to put his arm around her, or even take her hand.

The dorm lounge was empty. "Everyone's working on their projects," Didi said. "I guess I'll go into my room and see if I can grind something out. I'm supposed to be doing a short story about this girl I know who was on a plane that got hijacked. It's not coming very well."

"Were you ever hijacked?" Crunch asked.

"No, of course not."

"Maybe you ought to write about something that happened to you."

"Nothing's ever happened to me. Anyway, it's too late to change now. I'll press on. I'm not a writer anyway. I've learned that much at this place."

"Well, I never thought I was," Crunch said. "So I haven't suffered any disillusionment. At least," he added with a sigh, "not on that score."

"Are you going to do the project?"

"Maybe. But not now."

Didi wandered off to her room. The only sounds Crunch could hear were typewriters clacking behind closed doors. He supposed he could hang out with James and Meg. They wouldn't be working. But he didn't feel like it. He bought himself a soda, snapped on the TV, and sat down to watch another summer rerun.

The unexpected sound of the pay phone startled him. They all used it now and then to call out, but he'd never heard it ring with an incoming call. He didn't think anyone even knew the number. He picked up the receiver and said hello.

The man on the other end of the wire had a rich, deep bass voice with a fairly marked Eastern European accent. "Is this the dormitory at Hudson Manor?"

"Yes," Crunch replied.

"May I please speak to Eve Streitman."

"I'll see if she's in. Hold on." There was no answer at Eve's door. He tried Beth's.

"What is it?" Beth called.

"Is Eve there? She has a phone call."

Eve opened the door. Behind her, Crunch could see Beth, Rhonda, and Danny sitting on the floor amid typewritten sheets of paper, styrofoam cups, and soda bottles. Crunch figured they must have been reading the pieces they were working on to each other.

He followed Eve back to the lobby and sat down again in front of the TV, looking as if a coffee advertisement featuring the adventures of Juan Valdez was the most gripping drama he'd ever encountered. But what he was listening to was Eve's end of the conversation.

It didn't reveal much. "Hi . . . Oh, Dad, what's up?

131

Are you okay? . . . How about Mom? . . . Oh, good . . . I
. . . I . . . I'd rather not . . . No, really, please . . . Well,
of course it sounds lovely, but . . . Okay, I understand . . .
Friday around noon? . . . All right, I'll be ready." She
hung up the receiver with such a bang that Crunch no
longer merely pretended to be listening.

He rose from his seat. "What's the matter?"

Eve was staring at the phone. When she heard him
speak, she turned and faced him. "The matter? Nothing, I
guess."

"You almost yanked the wire out of the wall."

She was so upset she forgot she wasn't speaking to him.
"I can't stay till the end. They're picking me up Friday
morning."

"Who's they?"

"My parents, naturally."

"Oh. Why?"

"They were invited to Cape Cod for the weekend. They
thought I'd like it, so they're stopping for me on the way
up."

"Won't you like it?"

"I don't know. I love the beach, but there're no kids in
the house where they're going. I'd . . . I'd . . . well, I'd
really rather stay here, until the very end." She sounded
surprised by her own words.

"In spite of everything?"

"I don't want to miss the last things—you know, everyone's magnum opus, the cookout Friday night. . . ."

"So why didn't you just say so?"

"I did, kind of. But my dad said what difference does a
day make. And if I don't go, they won't go. It was tough
enough convincing them to let me come here for two

132

weeks. They'd never let me stay home alone most of Saturday and all day Sunday."

"Just over one night? What's the big deal? You're not five. You're fifteen."

"Well, they're kind of . . ."

"Strict?"

"Strict?" Eve repeated. "No, strict is the wrong word. Cautious? Afraid, maybe. Anyway, they just won't leave me. They never have. And I can't deprive them of a weekend they'd enjoy so much."

"Go up to the Cape Saturday. Take the train to Boston and the bus to Provincetown. They can pick you up there. The trip'll take all day, but so what—you're not so crazy to be there anyway."

A slow smile spread over her features. "Hey, Crunch, that's a great idea." Immediately she picked up the receiver and rapidly punched in the twenty-five digits required to effect a credit card call. "Dad?" she said. "I had a great idea." Her speech, Crunch noticed, was far more rapid than usual. She was allowing no time for interruptions. "You don't need to take the trouble of stopping for me. You can just pick me up in Provincetown late Saturday afternoon. I'll call you when I get in. The Boston train goes right through Vandyk's Crossing, and from there I'll take a bus to Cape Cod."

Crunch eyed Eve as she listened to her father's lengthy reply. Animation drained from her features. Gradually her shoulders sagged. "Yeah," she said quietly when he was done. "I understand . . . No, it's okay . . . Yeah, Friday morning . . . Okay . . . Bye." She hung up and turned to face Crunch. "No good. The people they're going to visit, the Cornicks, they're observant Jews. Dad says it would be inappropriate to show up at their place on a Friday night or Saturday. I should have realized that. I mean, I know the Cornicks."

Crunch shook his head. "I don't understand."

"They're Sabbath observers. They don't ride or cook or switch lights on and off or answer the phone or even write, from sundown Friday to sundown Saturday."

"But your family isn't that way, are they?"

"No, we're not. I mean, they send me to a Jewish school, and our home is kosher. We care a lot about being Jewish, especially my father, and we know a lot about it, but my parents aren't Orthodox the way the Cornicks are. If they were, they would never have let me come here."

Crunch remembered their conversation about keeping kosher during their very first cafeteria dinner. "But I still don't understand," he said. "If your family isn't so observant, why can't they pick you up in Provincetown?"

"My folks believe when you visit people you play by their rules. You know, when in Rome, do as the Romans do."

Crunch folded his arms across his chest. "Then just don't go, Eve. Just tell them you will not go. Tell them to have a wonderful time, you'll see them Sunday night." He'd said those very words to his own mother, and they hadn't worked. But two weeks was different from overnight. His parents had left him overnight at least half a dozen times.

"I can't do that," Eve said. "I just can't. If it were something really important, well, then, maybe. But it isn't important. In the grand scheme of things missing a cookout just isn't important."

"But it's what you want."

134

"Really, Crunch, so what? If you're not a baby, you don't need to get everything you want."

"Your parents sound like awful pricks to me. Though," he added magnanimously, "whose parents aren't?"

A warm pink flush overspread the smooth, pale, almost transparent skin of her face. To Crunch her delicate features appeared even more appealing than usual. "My parents are wonderful," she insisted. "They're the best people in the world. You don't know them, Crunch. So just don't say anything more about them." She strode purposefully across the room and started down the hall.

"Eve," Crunch called.

She didn't stop.

"Your parents, Eve."

Midstep she turned.

"Are they really so different from other kids' parents?"

"What happened to them was different. Just different," she said. "Can't you get that through your thick skull?"

"Things happen to everyone."

"Not like that. They're sad forever. There's no way they can be anything else."

"And it's your job to make it up to them?"

"I didn't tell you about my mother."

Oh, God, Crunch thought. Here it comes, another horror story.

She stepped toward him. "I never talk about these things, even with my friends at home. Why am I telling you?"

Maybe, he thought, because I'm the one who doesn't want to hear. But he knew he had no choice but to listen. Crouching, she leaned against the wall. He sat down on the floor opposite her. "My mother's ten years younger than my father, and she isn't Polish. She's Hungarian. She wasn't in a concentration camp. People out in the country hid her. Her aunt brought her there, kissed her, told her to be good, and left her. My mother never saw her aunt again. She never saw any of her relatives again. She was eight. She slept in the stable. The farmer and his family didn't love her; they scarcely spoke to her. But they gave her what they could to eat. One day the villagers heard that German soldiers were coming. They told the farmer to get rid of my mother. My mother was standing right there while they said it. 'Throw her in the dry well,' they said. 'Cover her with dirt.' My mother was sure she was going to die. And the amazing part of it was that she didn't feel anything. She didn't seem to care.

"But she didn't die. The farmer said, 'I was paid to keep her. I took money for her.' That's what he said. 'I took money for her.' " Eve looked at Crunch, as if to check his reaction. Crunch's face remained expressionless. Eve went on. "The peasant told my mother to burrow under the straw in the loft. So you see, she was sort of buried anyway. It turned out the report was just a rumor. The Nazis didn't come. But afterward, for years, my mother felt as if she were already dead. Even after she married my father and won prizes in physics and had me, she felt that way. She told me that's how she felt until my first birthday. They put me in my high chair and brought me a cake with a candle on it and sang to me. I laughed and clapped my hands. My mother told me that at that moment this utterly unexpected wave of feeling passed over her, a wave of fearful joy." Once again Eve raised her eyes to Crunch's. "Did you know you could be full of joy and full of fear at the very same moment?"

Crunch made no reply. He didn't think she meant for him to answer.

"That feeling didn't last," Eve continued, "though my mother says it's come back now and then. But at that moment she knew she was alive. She also knew why. I was the reason." Eve paused. "She lives for me. Now do you understand?"

He wasn't sure that he did. He'd have to think about it. And he knew he would, whether he wanted to or not.

Eve stood up and turned down the corridor back to Beth's room. Crunch rose too and hurried off to his own room. For the first time since he'd arrived at Hudson Manor, he opened the typewriter on his desk. He rolled a piece of paper into the machine. And then, with one hand, he began to type.

## THE GHOSTS OF MARYGROVE

A Short Story
by
Charles Oliver
July, 1988

# Second Wednesday

It was funny, Eve thought as she looked around the English resource room. No one had assigned them seats, yet for a week and a half, with few variations, they'd taken the same ones each morning. She'd noticed the same thing in classes at school. Sometime she'd write an essay about it. Against that day, she made note of the thought in her journal.

Enid opened the session with an announcement. "We've changed our minds," she said. "We *are* going to the Rockefeller church this afternoon."

"Does that mean all is forgiven?" Stu asked. On Monday, at the end of the formal session, Kent had announced that their punishment for Sunday night's incident was the cancellation of all plans for subsequent visitors and field trips.

Enid held a sheaf of papers in her hand. "The exercises

138

you did on Monday about what happened Sunday night were by and large extremely thoughtful. I think some of you still don't understand the enormity of what happened, but most of you seem to have learned from the incident. I don't think anything like it will be repeated. The punishment was meted out to the innocent as well as the guilty. In a situation like this one, there was no other choice." She stared at James. "By the same token, the unrepentant as well as the repentant will benefit from its recision."

"We don't want to make more of this than it's worth," Kent said.

"I have forgiven no one," Sierra announced.

"You're not expected to," Enid said.

Sierra lifted her chin. "Then why have you?"

"My dear Sierra," Enid returned quietly, "our position here is not your position. You are not us, we are not you."

Sierra turned to Eve. "What do you think?"

"It's all right with me," Eve said as loudly and as firmly as she could. She didn't want Sierra to think she was halfhearted in her response.

After lunch they piled into the van and drove to the Union Church in Pocantico Hills. A tiny place, capable of holding no more than a hundred worshipers, it was totally dominated by ten stained glass windows donated by the Rockefeller family. Awash in pale, colored light, the sanctuary seized Eve's heart like a vise. She sat in a pew, her notebook in her lap, unable, for a long time, to write a word. What could she say, in face of such glory, that would sound anything other than trite?

Beth, Danny, and Rhonda were scribbling rapidly. Martina was whispering to Linda and Didi. James was drawing; Meg was writing something beneath his pictures. Open notebooks rested in Crunch's and Stu's laps, but their eyes were shut. Sierra was strolling around the church with Enid and Kent, the descriptive pamphlets they'd picked up when they'd entered in their hands.

Nine of the windows were by Marc Chagall, and they were remarkable depictions of Old Testament prophets, the Good Samaritan, and the Crucifixion, in shimmering variegated blues, greens, and yellows. But wonderful as they were, it was not these windows that moved Eve the most deeply. The window that took her breath away was by Henri Matisse and it depicted nothing at all.

Though in the tradition of the rose windows that illuminate the altars of so many Gothic cathedrals, the design of Matisse's window was a total abstraction, created through cutouts that fit into an arabesque within the tracery of the window. Each panel was of a single unalloyed, vivid color—pure white, holy blue, vital green, and joyous yellow. Though together creating an utterly harmonious pattern, each of the cutouts was just slightly different in design. Absolute perfection had been achieved through the simplest, most economical of means.

With only half an ear, Eve listened to a guide describe the windows. She was too busy concentrating on seeing to spend energy on hearing. But she caught enough of what the woman was saying to learn that the window was Matisse's final creation. He'd never seen it installed, with the sunlight shining through it, except in his imagination. Bedridden, he'd created it with scissors and colored paper that assistants had arranged on the wall of his room according to his instructions.

Eve began to write. "When Matisse created the rose

window in the Union Church of Pocantico Hills, he was dying. He knew he was dying. Yet the window is as joyful a work of art as I have ever seen. It is a complete affirmation of life. Of course, Matisse died of natural causes in the fullness of his years. He was not cut off in his prime, and he was fully creative almost until the actual moment of his departure. Maybe that's why he could achieve such a piece even as he lay on his death bed. Still, I find it surprising."

Then she added a poem.

*Is hallelujah a color, Matisse?*
*Is it yellow or white,*
*Shards of glass like sunlight*
*Warming mortality?*

It was the best poem she'd ever written. She was sure of that.

Fourteen people in the van was too many, and they sat, as always, uncomfortably squeezed together. In the rear James was telling dirty jokes to Meg's, Crunch's, and Stu's appreciative howls. His voice was pitched just exactly low enough for Enid and Kent, who was driving, to miss the content of his remarks but catch their general tenor. The others chattered, strained to hear James, or slept. Eve managed to wrap herself in silence, as if she were alone on a seat in the back of a large, empty bus, and dream of Matisse's rose window.

Enid turned and shouted over the din. "Hey, you guys, don't forget. Give me what you've written as we get off the bus."

"It's rough," Didi complained. "Really rough."

"I know that," Enid said. "That's what it was supposed

141

to be—your spontaneous, unedited response to what you experienced."

The scrunch of pages being torn from notebooks filled the van as it pulled into the parking lot. Enid hopped off first and stood by the sliding door, her hand out. "James and I did ours together," Meg said.

"At least you did it," Enid returned, her smile taking on its Cheshire cat aspect.

"That church made me write a poem," Eve remarked as she handed her sheet to Enid.

"Me too," Crunch admitted. He was right behind her. Startled, Eve glanced at him. She'd never imagined he *could* write a poem. "I wonder if the people who go there every Sunday appreciate that church," he added.

"You get used to anything," Enid said. "But then something happens to make you see it new again."

Instead of loping off after they'd given her their work, they clumped around her as if they wanted, for a moment, to re-create the spell that had been broken on the ride home. "I'm not much for churches," Beth said, "but that one was a good place."

"A very good place," Rhonda agreed.

"I've lived around here all my life," Stu said, "and I never went there before. I don't know how I missed it."

"Thank you," Danny said. "Thank you for taking us there." He seemed to be speaking for all of them.

Kent stood on the steps of the van. Enid nodded to him, and he smiled back. Sierra said something to Enid, something Eve couldn't hear. The others moved off in a group, heading toward the dorm. For a moment Eve hesitated. Then, silently, she went with them too.

# Second Thursday

When she awoke in the middle of the night, Eve glanced at the clock. Two-fifteen. She climbed out of bed and opened her window. Moonlight bathed the campus in silver light. It was nearly as bright as day.

Slowly, as if in a dream, she slipped on a pair of shorts and some sneakers. She was already wearing a T-shirt. Then she opened the door to her room and stepped out into the hall. When she got to Crunch's room, she turned the knob as quietly as she could. It wasn't locked; none of them kept their doors locked. She tiptoed inside. His shade was open too; his room was engulfed in moonlight. On his dresser, next to his wallet and his sunglasses, lay keys. Rory and Bea had confiscated James's key to the padlock after Sunday night. They never realized Crunch had one too. She picked up his key ring, rattling it slightly. She glanced toward the bed; Crunch didn't even turn over. She slipped out of his room as silently as a cat. So far, so good.

But the door leading outside was a different matter. After Sierra's imprisonment, Rory and Beatrice had decided their curfew was insufficient. As a further precaution, they now locked the door every night from the inside. Only they had the key. Eve was sure that was against the fire laws, but so far no one had said anything about it. Maybe Kent didn't even know they were doing it.

There were stairs at the end of the hall—the ones she took to visit Rhonda, who lived on the second floor. She remembered now that from the same landing, another flight led to the cellar.

The basement was laid out much like the upper floor, and at the end of the corridor she found the door. It even bore an EXIT sign. She pushed against the bar and it opened. She tested the outside knob and found that it wouldn't turn without a key. It was a safety door, opening from the inside but not from the outside. She held it with her leg while she found a stone to prop it open. She intended to get back in without anyone's knowing she'd ever been out.

Her own foresightedness amazed her. As a matter of fact, everything she was doing amazed her. She moved slowly along the path leading to Marygrove. There was no rush. No one would see her at this hour of the night, but what if someone did? What difference could that make? They might delay her, that's all. They couldn't stop her.

At Marygrove she climbed down the cellar stairs, her little light barely penetrating the utter blackness of the corridor. She had resolved to come here, to the crypt, and she would hold to her resolve no matter how scared she was, down here alone, walking steadily toward the place she now understood to be in some sense the embodiment of her nightmares. She paused for a long moment before she pushed open the door to the room. And then she went inside.

She had left the outside door open. She would have liked to leave the door into the secret room open too, but its hinges were loose, and her foresightedness had not stretched to bringing along an extra rock with which to prop it open. She could use a shoe of course, or her notebook. But she didn't feel like walking across the moldy floor in bare feet, and she needed the notebook and the flashlight because she intended to write. So the door would have to remain closed. Perhaps it was better that way. It was a further test.

Settling down on the moth-eaten rug, Eve opened her notebook. For a long time she remained there, still as a statue, writing nothing. Her eyes were fixed on the sarcophagus. She could not stop staring at it.

After a while she got up. She moved across the room with heavy steps, as if she were walking through amber. When she reached the coffin, she ran her hand along the side. The stone was smooth and cold, granite she supposed. She put her fingers on the arm of the carved figure of Erastus Grove. The likeness wasn't skillfully done, but it projected a certain raw power. She gazed into the staring, protuberant, pupilless eyes. Then she knelt down, and putting her hands against the edge of the lid, she pulled at it with all her might. It didn't budge so much as a hair's width.

Suddenly she found herself bathed in a bright light.

Someone was standing in the doorway, carrying a flashlight ten times more powerful than hers. Blinded by the light, she couldn't tell who it was. He spoke; then she knew it was Crunch. "What are you doing?" he said.

"What does it look like I'm doing?"

"It looks like you're trying to open that coffin." He moved toward her, his light still directed in her face.

"That's right. Only I can't move it. I'm not strong enough"

"Let me help."

"You have only one arm."

"It's a wrestler's arm. Come on, we can try."

He stood next to her and assumed a position similar to hers. "Okay," he said. "Ready, set, go."

They heaved in unison. Eve thought she sensed a tiny movement. But it wasn't enough. The lid remained firmly closed. "If I had both arms, it would have worked," Crunch said. "I'll have to find something. I think I remember a piece of pipe from the time James and I explored all the rooms. Just wait a minute."

He hurried out, returning a moment later carrying a rusty spade. "I don't think the pipe would work," he said. "The end of it isn't thin enough to fit in the crack between the top and the bottom of the box. But maybe this will do the trick—if it doesn't break first."

Holding the end of the shaft, Crunch shoved the edge of the blade in the crack. "Now put both your hands around the stick," Crunch instructed.

Eve obeyed, tensing her body in preparation for Crunch's order to lift. But the order didn't come. Instead, Crunch said, "Are you sure you want to do this, Eve?"

"Do you?" she whispered.

"I'll do it if you still want to. But I'm scared. Really scared," he admitted.

"Yeah, so am I," Eve said. "That's why I have to do it."

He relaxed his hold on the spade for a moment. Following his cue, so did she. "You've got guts," he said. "You really do."

She shook her head. "No. I just told you, I'm scared."

"But that's what courage is—doing a thing you're scared to do. It's no trick if you're not scared."

"Oh." She smiled. "I hadn't thought of that." It was nice of him to say so.

"I'm scared before every wrestling match," he added.

"You said that the night you first brought us down here."

He lowered the spade to the floor and leaned on the handle. "It was a trivial secret, compared to the ones everyone else was telling."

She gazed at him steadily. "Tonight, how did you know I was here?"

"You told me you were coming. Don't you remember?"

"No. I didn't tell anyone."

"But you said maybe you had to find out who was really on that train in your dream."

"And from that you knew?" She found him more surprising with each word he uttered.

"Yes."

"How did you know I was here now?"

"You were in my room, weren't you?"

She nodded.

"I thought I heard someone in my sleep. I just figured out it was you. The keys were gone, so I checked your room. It was empty, and no one was in the bathroom."

147

"How did you get out? The front door is locked."

"Through my window. It opens onto Rory and Bea's apartment roof."

"Weren't you worried that they might hear you?"

"Weren't you worried that I might hear you?"

He was right, of course. Most everything worth doing involved some kind of risk. "Let's do it now," she said. "Let's open the box."

She watched as he reinserted the blade of the spade in the crack. "One," he intoned. "Two. Three. Lift!"

She pulled up with all the strength her two arms possessed. She felt as if she were trying to lift an entire pyramid. But the crack widened. The lid was moving. "Shove the spade through!" Crunch exclaimed. Together, they thrust forward, so that the blade was inside and the shaft rested between the lid and the container, forcing it to remain open.

Now Eve placed herself at one end of the coffin, and Crunch placed himself at the other. Once again she heaved and tugged, her body drenched in sweat. The lid swung upward; the hinges, unoiled for decades, creaked like old bones.

"Don't let go," Crunch warned. "The hinges might not hold."

The air rising from the box smelled ancient, unused. Eve couldn't help breathing it, but she didn't look down. Across the box, her eyes held Crunch's. He wasn't looking down either. "Who goes first?" he asked, his voice scarcely rising above a whisper.

"Let's do it together," she said.

"Okay." Again he counted. "One." With each number his voice grew stronger. "Two. Three. Look!"

Eve let her eyes fall away from Crunch's face. Out of

the corner of one of them she allowed herself to glance downward, wary as a deer prepared to run. And then, as the realization of what she was seeing pervaded her consciousness, she deliberately lowered her head and stared unblinkingly into the coffin.

It was empty. Empty, except for a bouquet of faded roses, tied with a white ribbon. The flowers had dried to the texture and color of pale parchment; the ribbon had turned yellow. Eve's breath alone was enough to shatter one of the blossoms into dust. "Let's close it," she said quietly, "before they all disappear."

Together, slowly, they lowered the lid. The hinges creaked, but they didn't break. "It will be easier for the next person," Crunch said. "He probably won't need a spade."

Eve's breath escaped her lips with a sigh. "Do you think there'll be a next person?"

"Maybe," Crunch said. "At next year's writers' workshop." He sat down cross-legged on the rug, facing the sarcophagus.

Eve sat down next to him. "I don't know about that. *I* had to open that box. It wasn't just idle curiosity."

"Tell me," Crunch said softly.

He needed to know, she thought, as much as she needed to tell. "The subway car in my dream is a coffin. And the person on it who's dead is me."

"But you're not dead," Crunch said.

"That's right, I'm not dead." For a moment she sat there silently, thinking. And then she spoke again. "All those things everyone imagined about the box, think of it. Every one of them was wrong."

"Which just goes to prove," Crunch said, "that what

this bunch imagines can be worse than reality. And better too, I suppose."

"That's not always true," Eve said. "Some things happen that are worse than anything any human being can imagine."

"You mean like what happened to your parents."

Eve nodded. "The thing you don't believe."

"I never said I didn't believe it." For a moment Crunch was silent. But he didn't look away. "I just didn't want to think about it. I'll tell you another secret about me, a real one this time. About a year ago the brat who lives next door was fooling around with my stereo, and he broke it. Well, I'm twice as old as he is, and more than twice as big. I hit him anyway. I hit him so hard he lost two teeth. I managed to convince myself it was no more than he deserved, and then I buried the whole incident as far down in the bottom of my mind as it would go, where I've buried all the other times I've hurt someone on account of my lousy temper. I don't like to think about that part of me. I don't like to remember what I've done when it's taken over."

"You have to remember," Eve said. "Otherwise it'll just happen again and again and again."

He nodded slowly. "There isn't anything worse than what some human being can imagine," he said quietly. "What happened to your parents was done to them by people. People thought it up; people imagined it. It isn't supernatural. It's all in people. Good and evil both. That's what I have to admit now. It's the truth I didn't want to face."

Eve shook her head. "I don't understand."

"You know those books I like, by Stephen King and those other horror guys?"

150

"I never read horror books," Eve said. "Like I never go to horror movies. I told you that."

"They're very popular with a lot of people besides me. I'll tell you why. It's because the evil in them is outside of people. Or if it's in people, some supernatural power puts it there. It's some force beyond their control. Lots of us would like to believe that's the way that it is. I was one of them. Now I know better. That's what I was really scared of—that recognition of what people can be—of what I can be."

"You mean Nazis were human beings."

"Yeah. That's exactly what I mean. Even Hitler was a human being."

"Oh, God." Eve buried her face in her hands.

"But so is Mother Teresa. She isn't a saint or a goddess. She's a human being. You see, that's what I've got to remember." He moved closer to her and put his hand on her shoulder. "You have to remember that too, Eve."

She shivered. He put his arm around her and pulled her close to him. His warmth was a comfort, and she allowed her head to rest next to his. "This room is full of ghosts," she said. "Not just Erastus's, not just Mary's." Tears were coursing down her cheeks. She hadn't expected tears; she rarely cried, and now she'd cried twice in one week. But this time she made no effort to hold her tears back. "That night everybody told what they were really, really scared of, except you."

"And you," Crunch reminded her.

"I told, later, the night you locked up Sierra. And you told, tonight. So now they're here—all our ghosts." She lifted her head from Crunch's shoulder and rose to her feet. "Let's leave them here," she said. "Let's go back now."

151

She reached out her hand. He took it, allowing her to help him up. Side by side they walked out of the room, down the corridor, up the stairs, and out into the balmy, light-streaked night. Eve lowered the door; Crunch snapped the padlock in place.

When they stood in front of her bedroom, he took her hand again and spoke to her in low, urgent tones. "Eve, did you really leave your ghosts in the crypt?"

She didn't answer immediately. She wanted to tell him the truth. "I don't know," she said at last. "As far as I could, I guess."

"Then when your parents come for you tomorrow morning, don't go with them."

"Oh, I have to go. I'm all packed."

"Eve, you can't spend your life making up to your parents for *their* ghosts. You can't!"

She pulled her hand away from his. "My parents are doomed to eternal sadness because they witnessed what is incomprehensible, inexplicable, and unbearable. You still don't understand that, do you?"

"I think I'm beginning to understand as well as anyone can who wasn't there."

"You don't," she returned sadly. "You don't." She opened her door. "Good night, Crunch," she said, and closed it behind her.

# Second Friday

Enid asked Stu to read his piece first. "No way," he protested. "Let Danny go first."

"Danny?" Beth exclaimed. "Please, not Danny. He should go last. Who could stand being compared with Danny?"

"That's why I think we should get his over with," Stu explained. "Then we don't have to sit around all morning digging our fingernails into our palms." He grinned at Enid. "Nice detail, huh? Nice and specific."

Enid licked the tip of her index finger and sketched a check mark in the air.

"You're all going to be disappointed when you hear my story," Danny announced. "Very disappointed." He seemed actually to mean it.

"Why don't we just draw lots?" Kent suggested. "That would be fairest."

Agreement was immediate, universal, and enthusiastic.

Eve ripped pages from her notebook and numbered them one through twelve. Rhonda removed the large straw hat she was wearing and held it out to Martina, who folded the scraps of paper Eve handed her and dropped them in. Stu passed the hat around, and each of them pulled a number.

"Who's got one?" Enid called out.

With a grimace Danny lifted his hand. Enid laughed. "Go ahead then," she said.

Danny had written a long short story, almost a novella. Eve had heard pieces of it before, in class, and late at night, in the dorm. He'd brought some parts of it with him from home, pieces he'd written for English classes over the previous three years. Other parts he'd written at Hudson Manor. But even though she was familiar with much of it, Eve was awed by the skill with which Danny had woven the sections together to create a unified coming-of-age story, in which the protagonist struggled to gain acceptance by the "in" crowd at the fancy summer camp he went back to year after year, only to discover, eventually, that "in" was not where he wanted to be. The story managed to be both sad and very funny at the same time, and it unfolded, more or less without commentary, through the vivid incident and detail that Enid had taught them to value.

Danny not only wrote well, he read well too. When he was done, they all applauded. "Oh, lord," Beth groaned. "I can't believe I have to go next." But Eve found her character study of a homeless man facing a Lake Erie winter vivid and deeply moving.

Actually, Eve thought, not one piece read in class that day was totally without some interest or value, even Didi's.

Her plan was too ambitious; trying to develop a whole airplane full of characters, she could only depict them through the shorthand of clichés and generalities. But at the end two passengers realized they were high school rivals who hadn't seen each other in thirty years, and that moment seemed real and touching.

Meg had produced a mere sketch of two or three pages, a scene at a party, but written with such wit and skill that Eve could imagine a whole novel rising out of it. She found Stu's endless account of the adventures of Albrecht the Outlaw so full of motiveless action and meaningless gore that she almost fell asleep during the reading. But fans of fantasy adventure applauded it enthusiastically, meaning, she supposed, that the fault was in her—she did not properly grasp the conventions of the genre.

"I have number six." James waved his scrap of paper in the air.

"Who has number seven?" Enid asked.

"Hold your horses!" James objected. "I've got something to read."

"You do?" Enid could not disguise her surprise. "All of a sudden you wrote something? Why?"

"When you print all these pieces in the *Hudson Manor Review*," James said, "I want to be there too. I want these guys to remember me."

"I'll tear out the pages you're on," Sierra snapped.

James ignored her and simply began reading. The animal caricatures he'd been drawing for two weeks became the characters in his brief, brilliant satire. Ostensibly set at a zoo, the real locale of his surrealistic fable was soon recognized by all to be the Hudson Manor Writers' Conference. At first Eve thought she was represented by the squirrel, and then it occurred to her that perhaps she was the mole. Her attention was focused totally on James, like everyone else's. She didn't hear the door open, or people enter the room. Not until James stopped reading in midsentence did she turn to see what he saw.

"Hello!" Enid said. "What can I do for you?"

Eve rose to her feet. "These are my parents," she said. She couldn't believe it was already time to go. She glanced at her watch. Not quite—only quarter of twelve. "Mom, Dad, these are our teachers, Enid Baswell and Kent Meckler. Kent, Enid—Micah and Elena Streitman."

Enid rose too and held out her hand. "It's indeed a pleasure to meet you. I'm familiar with your wonderful work, though I must admit I understand Herr Doktor Streitman's much better than I do Frau Doktor Streitman's."

"We are admirers of yours too," Eve heard her father say. She wondered if it was true, or if he was just being polite. "Eve has told us so much about you." That at least was a fact.

"Would you care to join us?" Enid turned back to the group. "Do you mind if Eve's parents listen to the remaining papers?"

I mind, Eve thought. I mind a lot. But she did not have to say it, which was a good thing, because she didn't think she could have said it. "Thank you very much," Micah Streitman replied. "It would be an honor indeed. But we cannot. We must be in Provincetown before sundown. We just stopped by to pick up Eve."

"Please forgive the interruption." Elena Streitman's voice was gentle, apologetic. "We thought Eve would be waiting for us at the dormitory."

"We're so sorry she has to leave," Enid said.

"Oh, well." Eve's father shrugged. "There are fewer than twenty-four hours left to the conference anyway."

"You're fifteen minutes early," Eve said. "That's why I wasn't waiting at the dorm." Not quite true. She was so absorbed in the class, which clearly was going to run over by at least an hour, that she had been utterly unconscious of the time. "Please, can't you wait just a few minutes? I want to hear the end of the story James is reading."

"Well, five minutes . . . " her mother said. "We'll wait outside."

"But Eve, you can't go," Crunch said. "We haven't heard *your* story."

"Yes, I know," Eve replied quietly. "And we haven't heard yours either."

"They're all to be published," Kent said.

"But the book won't be ready for months," Crunch said. "I want to hear Eve's story *now*." He glared at Eve's father.

Eve's father glared back. "I guess you'll just have to wait, young man."

"That's Crunch," Eve said. She continued around the circle, pointing. "Didi. Meg. James. Martina. Danny. Linda. Stu. Sierra. Beth. Rhonda."

"How do you do?" Dr. Streitman said. "I'm pleased to meet you. It would indeed be a pleasure to stay and get to know all of you better, but really, we must go—now."

"Dad?" Eve moved next to him.

"Yes?"

"I don't want to go." She spoke in a low voice; she didn't want to make a public scene. But it was a firm voice; they had to understand that she meant what she was saying. "Really and truly, I do not want to go."

157

Eve's mother peered at her through narrowed eyes, as if she were inspecting her for signs of a disease. Then she reached out and put her hand on her husband's arm. "Micah, Eve, let's go out into the hall and talk about this."

"I don't think there's anything to talk about," he replied. "Eve, let's go." Briskly, he walked out to the hall. Eve's mother followed. From the doorway, Eve turned and faced the group. "I'll be right back," she said.

Martina jumped to her feet. "Eve, you can come with me," she said. "I'm spending tomorrow night in New York City with my grandmother. Any friend of mine would be very welcome." Eve might have expected such an invitation from her buddies, Beth and Rhonda, but not from Martina. How surprising to discover that Martina understood so many things Eve had never told her. "Thanks, Martina," she said.

Closing the door behind her, she faced her parents. "Martina will let me stay with her tomorrow night," she said. "You'll be back Sunday."

"One day simply cannot be so important," Micah Streitman said.

"Yes, it is," Eve retorted. "As important as coming here in the first place."

"Then why didn't you say so?" her mother asked. "To begin with?"

"I thought I had." Eve felt tears well up behind her eyes. She could not say any more for fear that sobs instead of words would pour out of her throat.

Her mother kissed her, and touched her husband's hand. "Micah, we should let her stay. We should allow her to finish what we allowed her to start."

Her father stood staring at Eve, almost as if he'd never

seen her before. "Who is this Martina? Where does she live? Are you sure her family will permit a guest?"

"Martina's a wonderful girl. She's spending tomorrow night in New York with her grandmother, and she wouldn't have invited me if she didn't know it would be okay."

Micah Streitman opened his mouth as if he were about to speak and then covered it with his hand.

"It's settled then," Elena Streitman interjected quickly. "You'll call us on the Cape tomorrow night from the grandmother's house. Goodbye, darling. Have fun." She kissed Eve lightly on the cheek.

Her mother's words startled her father out of whatever dream he was dreaming. Briefly, his hand rested on Eve's head. "Make sure you don't forget that phone call."

"I won't."

He smiled a little. "Have fun," he said. Then he too turned and left.

Have fun. Have fun. They had each said it—two words she'd never heard issue from their lips in all her life. Eve opened the door and hurried back into the classroom. Maybe the train really had arrived in the station at last. Maybe she really was beginning to climb out of the car. "Thank you, Martina," she said. "Thank you very much."

She rejoined the circle, grateful it was not she who was to follow James. She needed time to recover her equilibrium.

Crunch held number seven. "I didn't finish," he explained, apologetically. "I realized what I needed to do too late to finish."

"That's all right," Enid said. "Read us what you've got."

"Meg's isn't finished either," Kent reminded him. "In the *Hudson Manor Review*, we'll label them 'works in progress.'"

Crunch's ghost story got no further than Mary Grove's

159

haunting by Erastus, and her decision to somehow confine the spirit who was disturbing her to a secret room. What he was going to do next remained a mystery, but everyone agreed that the story was appropriately atmospheric as far as it had gone. Eve wondered if he'd ever finish it.

Sierra's piece, polished to a high gloss, was about an encounter between an obnoxious, lonely old man and an equally lonely young punk in a video arcade. At the end Eve found herself shedding tears and feeling utterly furious at having been manipulated into them.

Then she had to read her own dumb story about Elmer Klampett's struggle with pigeon excrement. The laughter it generated was, she was sure, merely polite.

"Thank you," Enid said when she was done. "Eve, I wonder if in addition to your story, we might include the poem you wrote the day we went to the church in Pocantico Hills."

"That's more like it, isn't it?" Eve said.

"That and the piece you wrote the very first night," Kent said. "Not that the Great Pigeon Cleanup doesn't have many virtues."

"I like it," Rhonda said loyally. "I think it's very funny. And funny is good."

"You're talented, Eve," Enid assured her. "You just haven't found your voice. That's okay. You're very young. You're supposed to fool around with a lot of things before you settle in, like an art student copying old masters in the museum."

Eve wondered if Enid was telling her the truth. Danny and Sierra certainly seemed to have found voices. Meg and James were close too, though laziness and cynicism might prevent them from ever actually accomplishing anything. Or was it fear of not being good enough, a fear that they covered by putting down the whole enterprise?

160

"Hey," Stu said, "before we break up, I have to get everyone's address." He pointed to Enid. "Yours too."

"Don't worry," Kent informed him, "that's taken care of. Tonight at the cookout we'll give each of you a sheet with everyone's address. We figured you'd want them."

No one denied it.

Eve leaned against the balustrade of the veranda at Marygrove, her arms around Rhonda and Beth while Meg snapped their picture. "Thanks," Rhonda said as Meg returned the camera to her. "Now I'll take yours."

Meg made a face, but she stepped into Rhonda's place. "Come over here, James," Beth called. "Get in this picture."

Kent appeared, carrying a camera too. "Wait, wait," Martina cried. "I'm running back to the dorm to get mine." A picture-snapping orgy ensued, until finally Kent grouped them all on the lawn, mounted his camera on a chair, set the automatic timer, and ran around to an empty spot in the back row, arriving just in time. "One more," he said, repeating the entire operation.

"Will you make me a copy?" Eve asked. It had never occurred to her to bring a camera to a writers' conference.

"Everyone can have a copy," Kent assured her.

Stu carried out a tray of steaks, which he placed on the large grill in which he'd earlier built a fire. They ate at round tables on the porch, just as they had the first night. But it was so different, Eve thought. So different. Two weeks ago they had been strangers, wary of each other, even a little scared. Now they were—what? Not friends. Except for Martina over the weekend, she knew that if she saw any of these kids again it would merely be by chance. Forty years hence she might pass one of them on

161

Fifth Avenue and not even realize it. The snapshot would fade, and unless she identified them on the back, she would, for the most part, no more remember which name went with which face than she did for the picture of her nursery school class she'd come across in her mother's photo album.

But they'd gone through something together. A group had formed, it had broken apart, and then it re-formed in a different way, on different terms. Some of these people knew things about her that her closest friends at home didn't know. She couldn't, at first, think of a word to describe what they were to each other. Colleagues perhaps, colleagues for a little while.

After supper Enid and Kent presented each of them with a paperback copy of James Joyce's *Portrait of the Artist as a Young Man*. "Is this supposed to have some kind of significance?" James asked.

"It means whatever you want it to mean," Kent said.

"I probably won't even be able to get into it," Crunch said. "It's not by Stephen King."

"Try," Enid suggested. "You may surprise yourself—again."

Crunch smiled. "Thanks," he said.

"We have another surprise," Kent said. "We've been doing some writing ourselves. We'll read you what we've done."

"Remember the exercise about the boy getting off the bus?" Enid asked.

Didi nodded. "The same incident in three different styles—that was a killer."

"See if you recognize these styles," Enid said. She opened a folder and began to read.

162

He knew that if he stepped off the bus, he would fall eternally and forever through a blackness darker than black yet soft like clouds that billow up from dreams in which he can never rest but must always seek, seek following the trail of his soul until answers finally came.

Enid pushed on, lifting her voice above their delighted murmurs.

Answers, yes, answers to questions about why. But he knew that if he did not get off the bus, his mother would know what it meant to him, know what it meant to her, know what it meant. Stepping out into the nothingness, he tripped on his pinkie and heard the rumbling of distant thunder, or was it his mother's laughter?

He knew her laughter.

"That's me!" Martina exclaimed with a deep chuckle. "That is exactly me." She was clearly pleased, and she had a right to be, Eve realized later, after Kent and Enid had read some of the others. The takeoffs that worked the best made fun of kids who had enough personal style to satirize. Kent read next.

You're either on the bus or you're off it. That's what I say. Right now I was on it, but I was so far at the back that I might as well not have been there. When we pulled into the Port Authority terminal, I knew I had to find my way out. I had been on the bus long enough. Too long. It felt like every summer since I was ten. I walked down the aisle. I turned to say "Hi" to the wimp on the second doubles team and failed to see the soccer goalie's Reeboked foot shoot out in front of me. I tripped and fell flat on the seat of my white flannel trousers rolled at the cuff, while in my ears I could hear the mermaid lilt of Lorelei's laughter.

"Danny!" Stu shouted gleefully. "T. S. Eliot references and all. Now read mine."
Enid obliged.

The bus pulled up to the bus station in the middle of the dark wood. Albrecht agilely leaped off, even though weighted down with three knives stuck in his high black boots, three more stuck in his brace, a battle ax strapped to his back, and a shining sword with a talking jeweled hilt. Unfortunately he was thrown off balance by these deadly instruments of death and tripped on a half-eaten Snickers bar. A princess passing through the waiting room contemplated the scene with amusement, and much to Albrecht's mortification, she smiled. The insult was more than a man of Albrecht's character could bear. "Whoreson," cried the talking sword hilt, "are you going to let that pass?"

"Course not," Albrecht responded, and he ran her through.

She died.

When Kent began reading, Eve had no difficulty recognizing herself.

Elmer Klampett spent most of his time on the bus nervously watching other passengers drop wads of used chewing gum, candy wrappers, and snot-filled tissues on the floor. More and more garbage every day. Where was the city going to put it? At his stop, he tripped on an orange peel. A pretty girl laughed at his plight. "This is serious," he shouted. "Garbage is serious." By the time he had regained his footing, the girl had disappeared down a manhole. He followed her underground. She was gone. In her place was a subway car. Or was it a box? A box or a subway car? How many times had he seen whatever it was in his soiled dreams? Dare he look in it? Dare he not look in it? Would the girl be in it? Or would he instead see only the filthy flotsam and jetsam of the city's streets? Elmer didn't want to know the answer to that question. He turned and left the subway behind forever.

James was laughing so hard he was clutching his stomach. Crunch caught Eve's eye, and she managed to return his smile, even though she knew there were some things, like her dream, that she would never really find funny. It was all right if the others laughed. She'd changed enough to be glad they could. But she'd never be entirely free of the past. Who was, after all? That was all right too. In spite of what being their daughter meant, she didn't want any parents other than the ones she had.

A short while later, Enid kissed them all and climbed into her ancient VW Bug. They stood in a clump on the lawn and waved as she drove away.

"I guess the party's over," Linda said.

"Not quite," Stu said. He took her hand, and they wandered off.

Meg and James disappeared too. Crunch and Danny hung out with the girls, who took a walk along the river—all of them, even Sierra. Eve had thought they'd be up all night, but the airport limo was expected at six in the morning. By midnight they said good-bye in the lounge and went to bed, whether they had a plane to make or not.

Linda was right. The party was over.

# Second Saturday

The van was scheduled to return from the airport to cart the remaining conferees to the station in time to catch the eleven-eighteen from Vandyk's Crossing to Manhattan. Eve was in her room contemplating her notebook when she heard a knock on the door. "Who's there?" she called.

"Crunch."

She was not surprised. She knew they still had something to say to each other. "Come on in," she called.

His broad frame filled the doorway. She looked up into his face. "Can I sit down?" he asked.

"Of course." Imagine his asking, she thought. He took the bed. She placed herself opposite him, in the chair.

"Listen," he said, "I want to tell you something. I wanted to invite you to come home with me, to New Jersey. It's just that Martina beat me to it. But I thought

167

maybe you would come anyway. I think Martina would understand."

"Thank you, Crunch. Thank you very much. But I'm going to go with Martina."

"Lenape's not very far from New York. Forty minutes on the train."

"I know. I'm still going with Martina." She said it as gently as she could.

"What I mean is, I could come in sometime—you know, to see you." He was gazing down at the cast on his arm as if he expected it to signal some secret message.

She rose from the chair and sat down next to him on the bed. "No," she said softly, "I don't think so."

He lifted his head. "After all of this, it's hard to believe you still don't like me." There was a certain matter-of-factness to his tone, which, she realized, covered not anger but pain.

"I like you very much, Crunch. Believe me, I do. But you have to understand. To go to the theater on the Sabbath, to eat food that isn't kosher—that's one thing. To get involved with a boy who isn't Jewish—that's another."

"You can't do that to *them*?" he asked.

"I don't think I can do that to me either," she replied.

"I don't understand."

"It's hard to understand," she agreed. "But I don't want to begin what I could never finish. It wouldn't be fair to either of us."

He shook his head. "That's crazy. I'm not asking you to marry me." He grabbed her shoulder and turned her toward him. "You don't like me. That's the real reason. It has to be."

One minute he was more mature than most grown-ups

she knew, and the next minute he was a spoiled child. "Is that what you think?" she said, rising from the bed. "Look, Crunch, I'm going to show you something." She picked up her notebook and handed it to him. "This is my journal. You're the first person I've ever shown it to."

He glanced at the page. "I wrote everyone's name down the first day I was here," she explained. "Then I wrote what I thought of them. See over here? That's the space for the revised opinion I was supposed to put in today. But I found out I couldn't fill in the blanks. There was too much to say. I wrote this instead."

She pointed to the entry that began underneath the chart. He read it slowly, and her eyes followed his as once again she absorbed the words she had written.

I can't believe the blind complacency of the characterizations I so blithely scribbled on this page a mere two weeks ago. If I'd learned nothing else here, I'd still have found out that the only people you can sum up in three smart-alecky phrases are people you don't know very well. Once you get underneath the surface, a person who at first glance seems simple, even shallow, turns out to be unbelievably complicated. It would take me weeks to write the truth about the people I met at Hudson Manor. I doubt that I'll ever do it.

Just for an example, take Crunch. I thought he was merely a self-satisfied, carefree jock, without feeling or sensitivity. He was like a dream teenager in a TV ad for designer jeans. I hated him.

169

But no one did more for me here than Crunch. Though it was a painful experience for him, he took the trouble to find out who I was and to help me to see it too. He didn't want to, but his own better self won out over the ostrich part of him, the part of him that wanted to go on hiding his head in the sand. I may not be able to write about every person at Hudson Manor, but I hope that I'll soon be able to tell the story of the night Crunch and I spent alone, except for our ghosts, in the crypt of Marygrove.

I taught Crunch that you can't escape the evil in human beings. He taught me that the evil doesn't have to blind you to the good.

I will never see him again. But I will never forget him as long as I live.

Crunch laid the journal down beside him, and then turned and looked at Eve. "That last line," he said. "Ditto for me."

"Will that do?" she asked gently.

"It will have to," he said. With his good arm he pulled her toward him, and then he kissed her, a long, lingering kiss on her lips. She did not resist. She didn't want to.

He stood up. "Good-bye, Eve," he said.

"Good-bye, Crunch," she replied. "Good-bye, friend."

Then he was gone. Alone, she shoved the notebook into her open suitcase. She thought she might cry, but she concentrated on Crunch's kiss instead. She'd never let a boy get close enough to kiss her before. So Crunch's kiss had been the first.

A lovely thing, a kiss. But she'd found something even lovelier at Hudson Manor. She'd tasted freedom. She didn't need to reject her parents or their past in order to be free. She could never do that. On the contrary, she had to look at them straight, without flinching. And then she had to say, "You must live with your memories as best you can. But I have to live my way."

Well, when she called them later, she wouldn't say that, not exactly. She'd simply tell them she was fine, just fine.

## ABOUT THE AUTHOR

BARBARA COHEN is a graduate of Barnard College and has also received an M.A. from Rutgers University. She is the recipient of the Association of Jewish Libraries's Sydney Taylor Body-of-Work Award. Among her popular books for young adults are *Roses, Lovers' Games,* and the Bantam Starfire novel *People Like Us*. She and her husband live in Bridgewater, New Jersey, and have three grown daughters.

# Temple Israel

**Minneapolis, Minnesota**

IN HONOR OF THE 80TH BIRTHDAY
OF
ROSE SCHLEIFF
BY
HER FRIENDS